DEATH ON THE DEVIL'S HIGHWAY

Innocent, yet sentenced to hang for a murder, mustang man Auggie Kellerman escapes from custody hoping to clear his name. But now he's fair game for every lawman, bounty hunter, and Indian-tracker in the Arizona Territory. He's also a target for the 'Copper King', Charlie Keogh, who stands to lose everything if he makes it back alive. Now, he must ride the Devil's Highway, a harsh and dangerous trail — and administer some six-gun justice to save his reputation.

JOSH LOCKWOOD

DEATH ON THE DEVIL'S HIGHWAY

Complete and Unabridged

LINFORD
Leicester

First published in Great Britain in 2011 by
Robert Hale Limited
London

First Linford Edition
published 2013
by arrangement with
Robert Hale Limited
London

A catalogue record for this book is available
from the British Library.

ISBN 978–1–4448–1671–6

Published by
F. A. Thorpe (Publishing)
Anstey, Leicestershire

Set by Words & Graphics Ltd.
Anstey, Leicestershire
Printed and bound in Great Britain by
T. J. International Ltd., Padstow, Cornwall

This book is printed on acid-free paper

1

Arizona Territorial Prison, July 1879

A tiny cactus wren came to rest on one of the strap-iron crossbars that made up the cell door, took a quick peek inside, and flicked away toward the cotton-woods along the Gila River.

'Quick learner,' Auggie Kellerman muttered. 'And I'm next.'

His cellmate, a heavy-jowled German named Benjamin Martz, snorted softly behind him. 'I thought you were riding out today.'

'Yeah,' Kellerman said with a somber nod. 'They're hauling me back to Tucson to hang for a crime I didn't commit, and I'm not real anxious to go.'

'Hell, man,' Martz murmured, 'half the cons in here will swear up and down they never committed a crime.

1

Those Mormon boys, now, most of them are here for sleeping with some girl after promising to marry her and then backing out of the deal, but between me and you and the piss-pot, I think they're secretly a little proud of their exploits.'

Auggie rubbed a work-hardened hand over the stubble of his beard and stepped back into the shadows of the already stifling cell.

'Well, I really didn't do anything,' he replied. 'The only reason I'm here is because there's copper on my spread and some fat cat from San Francisco wants to be richer than he already is.'

'Ain't that always the way of it?'

The clacking of doors being unlocked down the cell block came to them then, guards issuing orders, and they waited as patiently as they could for their own turn to be let out.

'You got a plan?' Martz asked quietly.

Auggie lifted his hands in resignation and glanced around over his shoulder. 'No, but if I get a shot I'll have to take it. For damned sure I'm not going to just sit on my duff and let them stretch my neck for something I didn't do.'

'Can't blame you none for that.'

It was a few minutes before their door swung open and the turnkey motioned them to step out.

'Kellerman,' he rumbled, 'you're riding out today. You report to the main sallyport after breakfast. Martz, you draw a hoe from the tool shed. You'll be working in the fields.'

'Suits me.'

Martz planted a big hand in the middle of Auggie's back and shoved him out into the gathering heat of the day ahead of himself with a lopsided grin working its way across his ruddy face. 'Wonder what's for breakfast.'

'Does it matter?' Auggie mumbled.

They fell into the line of prisoners trudging off toward the mess hall across the hard-packed caliche yard then, nodding to the ones they knew and sizing up those they didn't. It was coming on to be hotter than the hubs of

3

hell today and there was not a smile to be seen.

The heady smells of strong coffee and fresh-baked bread assailed their nostrils the instant they stepped into the room and they filed through the serving line, holding out chipped enamel plates and tin cups for their portions.

After a night of forced silence in the cells the inmates already at the tables were gabbing among themselves almost non-stop, wolfing their food down and swilling coffee in hopes of staving off the effects of dehydration during their day's work.

Guards with critical eyes and sawed-off 12-gauge shotguns lined the walls, watching for any untoward move, but nothing happened and the morning meal was over all too soon.

'Don't guess I'll be seeing you again, Auggie,' Ben said at his shoulder as they paced out. 'I've still got a little time to serve then I'm heading north.'

'What's up north?'

'A cooler climate for one thing. And my son, of course. I haven't seen him in so long he probably won't even recognize me.'

'Now that's something to ponder,' Auggie answered.

'Anyway, best of luck to you, big guy. I hope you get your chance.'

'So do I.' Auggie offered his hand to the burly German, proud and a little sad when Martz gripped it. 'Take care of yourself, Ben. Nobody's going to do it for you.'

Martz nodded his agreement. 'I reckon that's right. Good knowing you, Auggie.'

He turned away then and fell in with the other cons heading for the tool shed, and Auggie started for the sallyport.

A surge of hopelessness washed over him as he paced toward the narrow sallyport gate, and there was precious little he could do to ward it off.

It had all the earmarks of being a long damned day.

The mustachioed guard, toting a .44–.40 Winchester, sitting in the shade of the sallyport, closed one eye and squinted at him with the other when he stepped up close.

'August Kellerman,' Auggie said automatically. 'Riding out.'

'Turn around.'

He lifted his arms, turning slowly until he faced the guard again, and waited.

'I guess you're clean,' the guard muttered. 'Hold out your hands.'

He did as he was told and the guard snapped a pair of shiny steel handcuffs around his wrists.

'Now your feet.'

Again he obeyed the guard, standing very still while the guard clapped the chained leg-irons around his ankles.

He unlocked the outer gate then and jerked his head toward the prison's ornate black and yellow tumbleweed wagon — a standard freight wagon with a simple iron cage bolted to the bed — standing in the scant shade of the wall.

'You start any ruckus out there,' the stocky guard intoned, 'that Lowell battery gun in the tower up there will be more than happy to spray you down with six hundred rounds a minute.'

'I could have gone all day without hearing that,' Auggie droned.

'You get my meaning, though?'

'Yeah, I get it.'

'All right then. Climb in.'

Auggie didn't reply, just shuffled across to the rear of the wagon and hoisted himself up into the cage.

'Give my regards to the hangman,' the guard rasped behind him with a thinly disguised smirk spread across his lips.

'You know where you can stick your regards.'

The two prisoners already sitting shackled in the back of the tumbleweed wagon had a mean look about them and he knew them only by reputation.

The bulky one with fists like a Virginia ham was big Jim Melnick and word around the yard was he'd kill you as soon as look at you. His thighs were thick, his face wide, desert dark, and he seemed to have a perpetual sneer.

The other, Ira Davis, was a half-breed Apache who had no use for anyone. The Apaches had rejected him as being an *indaa*, a white-eye, and the anglos wouldn't trust him for a minute.

'You the guy who's getting hung in Tucson?' Melnick asked, peering at Auggie with hooded eyes as he climbed in.

'That's what they tell me.'

'You don't seem very concerned about it,' the beefy convict muttered half under his breath. 'Something going on we should know about? Somebody meeting you on the road?'

Auggie shook his head but didn't look away. 'No, nothing like that. It's just that these bastards hold all the cards.'

'Well, we got dates with a hangman, too,' Melnick ventured. 'Back in Texas. So if you've got something going, you need to let us in on it. That hanging business sticks in our craws real bad.'

Davis chuckled at his words, the laugh-lines at the corners of his eyes suddenly showing up as wrinkles.

'Trust me,' Auggie mumbled, 'there's nothing cooking.'

He mopped the sweat off his face on the sleeve of the coarse black-and-grey striped uniform they'd given him, leaned back against the bars of the cage, and fell silent.

It was several minutes before the marshal showed up, a slope-shouldered man with a shock of unruly brown hair and a little bit of a pot belly. Probably had a wife and a couple of tow-head kids waiting for him somewhere, too, Auggie judged.

'How's things, Eli?' he asked the cynical sallyport guard.

' 'Bout the same, Jack. How're you doin'?'

'So far, so good,' the marshal said flatly. He nodded toward the men sitting uncomfortably in the back of the wagon, and held out his hand for the ring of keys. 'These the prisoners?'

'That's them. One August Kellerman, going back to Pima County to hang for murder; James Melnick and Ira Davis, both going to Texas. They none of them got anything left to lose, so watch your back.'

'Kellerman going to Tucson?'

'Yep. Pima County jail. Your canteens are full and there's grub and coffee under the seat.'

The marshal bobbed his head, clanged the barred door of the cage shut, and snapped a lock through the heavy iron hasp.

'Good enough,' he replied. 'See you next trip.'

He tied his horse, a long-legged sorrel with a white blaze on her forehead, to the rear of the wagon, paced slowly forward, and climbed up on to the seat using the spokes of the wheel as a ladder.

'I had a bad night last night, boys,' he said over his shoulder, 'so don't get cute with me today. I'd just as soon put a .45

10

slug between your eyes as take any of your guff.'

He slapped the long reins down on the rumps of the big-footed draft horses then and the wagon jerked forward with an awkward lurch.

'You got a name?' Auggie asked his back.

'Name's Jack Raley,' he said without turning. 'Deputy US Marshal Jack Raley. And don't get the idea that makes us long-lost buddies or something, 'cause it don't.'

Auggie snorted softly at his words. 'Never hurts to have friends.'

He glanced around then and found big Jim Melnick squinting at him with suspicious eyes. He met his look evenly.

What was that all about?

The marshal swung the wagon around the corner of the prison, away from the scraggly trees in the yard and out of sight of the Lowell battery gun, skirted the eighteen-foot-high west wall, and started down the steep road to the baked streets of Yuma.

'I don't make friends with condemned men,' the deputy muttered. 'No future in it.'

'You married?'

'Why don't you just button your tater trap, Kellerman? We got no reason at all to get acquainted.'

Auggie cocked his head at the rebuff, fully aware that the deputy couldn't see it. 'Just thought you might like a little conversation.'

'Well, I don't, so let it go.'

'Whatever you say. You're the deputy.'

Raley bobbed his head ponderously and slapped the reins down on the rumps of the team again, urging them into a shambling trot on the dusty road.

'And don't you forget it.'

'You a real friendly dude, ain't you?' Melnick rasped at Auggie.

'Not so's you'd notice,' he said, 'but if I can get this guy to relax a little . . .'

The stocky con nodded his understanding then and grinned. 'Let us know if you need any help when the time comes. Me and Ira are real good at helping out.'

Auggie turned away from them, studying the dense mesquite thicket south of the Army post on the bluffs across the river, realizing that, if he could escape, California would be a real possibility for dropping out of sight.

The trail, through Yuha Well and northwest to the coast, was well known and supposedly easy to follow.

The thought went against everything he believed in, though, and even as he considered it he knew he'd never take it.

No, his route lay to the east.

The system had wronged him and it was up to him to set it straight.

The barren swell of Prison Hill blocked his view to the west as they turned on to the old Gila River road, away from the sprawling settlement that was Yuma, and he scanned the desert ahead of them with a wary eye.

The land rose to the east, rocky and dry, cluttered with cholla cactus and sage, and there was no shelter at all from the blistering sun.

'I was married once,' the deputy mumbled finally. 'She died of cholera and that's when I gave up on ranching and became a lawman.'

'Sorry to hear that,' Auggie replied. 'The part about your wife, not about you becoming a lawman. That must have been tough.'

He was aware the two other prisoners were watching him, apparently trying to read something into his banter with the marshal, and he could have told them up front there was nothing to it.

Just a gambit to loosen the man up.

'Everything's tough out here,' the deputy droned. 'You just have to rise above it.'

'Yeah, well, they say a man's like a watermelon. You can never tell how good he is until he gets thumped a few times.'

Raley twisted on his seat then and peered at him through the bars of the cage. 'Looks like you got thumped a few times recently.'

'Trust me,' Auggie replied, 'it doesn't happen often.'

2

Auggie had nothing against the deputy — didn't even know him, really — it was just that he was wearing regular clothes and had that big Colt Peacemaker riding low on his hip.

He didn't seem like a bad guy as far as US marshals went, he just had the misfortune of being in the wrong place at the wrong time.

Raley pulled the tumbleweed wagon off the road into the shadow of some split red rocks just east of the Gila Mountains, and stepped down from the driver's seat. Auggie watched him through the bars of the cage as he put together a small fire of mesquite branches and dry ocotillo wands.

'I've got to pee, Deputy,' he mumbled from the tiny cage.

'Pee your pants.'

'Oh, for Christ's sake, man,' Auggie

16

groused, clutching the bars. 'You're taking me back there to hang by the neck until dead in front of half the damned town and you know it. Leave me a little dignity, will you?'

Raley studied him through the bars for a long minute then, considering it, and finally nodded his head.

'Yeah, you're right,' he said evenly. 'A man shouldn't have to die smelling like stale piss.'

He fished the heavy keyring out of his pocket, unlocked the door, and motioned for Auggie to clamber down.

'What about us?' Melnick grumbled through the bars.

'You can wait.' He locked the cage door shut again, turned back to Auggie, and nodded toward the flats. 'Over there in the sage where I can see you.'

Auggie snorted loudly at his words and held his manacled hands up for the deputy to see. 'What?' he asked insolently. 'You think I'm going to run?'

'Just get on with it.'

He shuffled a few steps away, into the

sage and teddy-bear cholla, not quite believing the deputy had actually let him out of the cage. As far as he was concerned, that was the deputy's mistake.

If you couldn't read a bluff as obvious as his had been, you shouldn't be buying chips.

Especially not in a game where a man was playing for his life.

He waited silently while Raley staked the long-legged sorrel in a thin patch of mesquite, leaving her to forage for the fat tornillo beans on her own, and set a coffee pot down on the rocks next to the fire to heat up.

Without a word Auggie hitched his black-and-grey striped prison-issue trousers back up, doubled the shackle chain that dangled so noisily between his wrists, and swung it hard at the back of the deputy's head.

It wasn't a killing blow, he knew that, still the man wilted as if he'd been pole-axed.

He hadn't liked doing it that way, but

then again he had no desire to test the business end of a hangman's noose, either.

Wasting no time, he rolled the deputy on to his back, knelt over him, and fished the heavy keyring out of his pocket.

It took him a few minutes of trying different keys before he found the right ones and he set to work removing the shackles. The cuffs came off first, then the leg-irons that had been clapped so tightly around his ankles, and he was free.

'Turn us loose, Kellerman,' Davis growled through the bars. 'You can't just leave us sitting here like this.'

'I can,' he said, 'but I won't.'

He tossed the ring of keys into the cage and narrowed his eyes at the other two. 'Turn yourselves loose. I've got my own problems.'

He set the deputy's gunbelt to one side, tugged the man's trousers off one leg at a time, a little surprised he was wearing long johns in this kind of heat, then stripped him of the faded maroon shirt and his sweat-stained hat.

'What about him?' Melnick asked, climbing down from the bed of the wagon and nodding toward the deputy.

'What about him?' Auggie countered.

'We've got to take him out to give ourselves a little time.'

Auggie shook his head, glancing up at them. 'No, we're not doing that.'

'Why not? He's nothing to us.'

'No, he's not,' Auggie agreed, 'but he hasn't done anything wrong, either. Just doing his job.'

The half-breed picked a chunk of broken rock up from the desert floor then and paced forward toward the fallen marshal with a murderous look working its way across his face.

'Nobody asked you,' he rasped raising the rock.

Without a second's hesitation, Auggie slid the marshal's Peacemaker out of its worn holster and lifted it toward Davis.

'I said we're not doing that.'

He waited long enough for Davis to

lower the rock, then continued. 'You two can unhitch the team if you want and ride out of here on them. I'm keeping the sorrel.'

'Why do you get the sorrel?' Melnick asked angrily.

'Very simple, big guy . . . I've got the gun.'

'You just made yourself some enemies, Kellerman. The kind that won't forget whose side you're on.'

'I'll worry about that when the time comes,' he replied.

'I've got a bad habit of holding a grudge for a long time.'

'And I've got a bad habit of fighting back.'

Melnick turned toward the half-breed and bobbed his head. 'Nothing more to be said then. Let's ride.'

Auggie watched them warily as they unharnessed the team of heavy draft animals, led them out of the traces, and climbed aboard.

'Any ideas?' Melnick asked his wiry riding partner.

'Nothing to worry about, Jim,' Davis responded. 'My mother showed me places in the desert the white-eyes don't even know exist. We can hole up out there for as long as we want.'

They rode out then, heading north toward the Gila River, and Auggie watched them until they were out of sight behind a low hill some distance away.

Satisfied he was safe for the time being, he holstered the Colt again and turned his attention back to the unconscious marshal.

He shucked out of the coarse prison uniform they'd given him in Yuma, quickly donned the deputy's clothes, strapped the gunbelt around his own waist, and paced away toward the sorrel.

Oh, he'd go back to Pima County, all right.

Only not the way they'd expected.

There was a man back there he wanted to run into again in the worst kind of way . . . paunchy Charlie Keogh

. . . his no-scruples, big businessman neighbor in the rocky Ajo Valley.

Keogh was the self-proclaimed Copper King of Arizona, the man who sent tons of ore on ox carts from the mines at Ajo to the Colorado River at Yuma and sent them on, by barge and ship, to a smelter overseas. He was the big money-man in town and had no qualms at all about showing it, smoking fat Havana cigars and standing everyone a drink at the saloon.

He was a squat, powerfully built man. The kind you didn't want to get close to in a fist fight. The kind Auggie purposely avoided, except, in this instance, he hadn't had a choice.

The man had set him up to take the fall for a murder he himself had committed — one of the prettiest damned frame jobs Auggie had ever heard of — and that was the part that chafed him.

He was no angel by any stretch of the imagination and, if he'd done something wrong, could accept the punishment that followed as something he had coming.

But in this case he hadn't done anything wrong, and he didn't have it coming.

There was no way in hell he deserved the punishment they'd doled out to him and he damned sure wasn't going to hold still for it.

He climbed into the saddle and glanced up the rutted wagon road toward Tucson. It ran alongside the Gila and Santa Cruz Rivers for much of its length, promising shade under the cottonwoods, unlimited water and forage, but it was a well-traveled road with freight wagons moving back and forth and settlers coming west. It was a lead-pipe cinch he'd be seen if he took it and that was the one thing he wanted to avoid.

He twisted in the saddle, studying the wide expanse of the Lechuguilla Valley, studded with glistening clumps of teddy-bear cholla and the tall spikes of saguaro cactus jutting up above the desert floor. A few yards away a jackrabbit with translucent red ears sat watching him, and high overhead a lone Sonoran buzzard swung in great, lazy circles against a cloudless sky.

Thirty miles to the south, he knew, was the water at Tinajas Altas, the High Tanks, and the parched trail of El Camino del Diablo, the Devil's Highway, running southeast.

He knew, too, it would be shorter to ride that way, but it was not a trip any man in his right mind looked forward to. It meant running from one water hole to the next, some of them not even on the map, with no guarantee there'd be water in any of them. And, without water in that untamed land, he would be toying with death itself.

Eighty years before the Mayflower landed at Plymouth Rock, Spanish explorers had traveled that trail, and during the gold rush days thousands of would-be prospectors had charged into its insane heat in a dash for the riches of California.

Many of them had died within a few feet of water, either not knowing it was there or too weak to climb up to the tanks; the dusty path across the desert was lined with their graves.

It was a piss-poor reputation for a trail to have, but that was the reality of it.

There was no doubt in Auggie's mind that once the deputy came to and could make his way back to Yuma the telegraph wires beside the wagon road would be alive with news of his escape.

By sundown every lawman and bounty hunter in the Territory would be out gunning for him. Quechan Indian trackers, whom he wouldn't be able to shake, would be on his ass in a matter of hours trying to earn the fifty dollars the prison system paid them for the return of escaped convicts.

Worse than that was the fact that Charlie Keogh would know he was coming. And that was the very last thing he wanted.

Still it had to be done, and the old

Camino del Diablo trail was by far his best bet.

He tugged the sorrel's head around to the south, heeled her into a ground-eating canter, and started down the valley without so much as a backward glance.

He'd been to the tanks once before, on his first trip west, and, even though he remembered the nine cup-like pools of water, strung one above the other like a chain of beads in that precipitous cleft of granite, it had been a long time since he'd been there and he wasn't at all sure he'd recognize the narrow canyon again when he came to it.

He had no choice but to find it.

The Tinajas Altas was the only reliable water for the next fifty miles.

3

He smelled the wood smoke long before he spotted the fire, and reined in among the boulders at the side of the wash.

'Hello the camp,' he called out. 'All right to come in?'

'Who are you and what do you want?' came a man's voice from the shadows.

'Passing through,' Auggie replied. 'Just wanted to water my horse.'

'Auggie?'

His forehead furrowed into a frown then and he realized with a sudden shock that he knew the voice. It was Joey Benitez, his long-time foreman at Ajo and one of the best bronc busters he'd ever known.

'Joey?' he asked into the semi-darkness. 'What are you doing here? I heard in Yuma that Keogh's men had raided the ranch and killed everyone.'

The slightly built Mexican foreman stepped into the firelight then, peering at him and lowering the double-barreled scattergun in his hard hands.

'It's true, *jefe*. They surprised us early in the morning and we didn't have a chance. Ten or twelve of them, and they were angry at what they'd been told about you killing Garza.'

'I didn't kill him, Joey.'

Joey bobbed his head and fed an ocotillo wand into the guttering fire. 'I knew that. Never believed it for a minute. It just wasn't your way.

'We had to get out, my family and I,' he continued quietly. 'I buried all the men, made crosses for their graves, and ran the horses into that little box canyon south of the ranch, but Keogh's men came down a few days later and burned us out.'

'Burned us out?' Auggie winced at Joey's news, remembering how hard they'd worked building the place.

'*Sí*. Everything. Even the crosses I made. They ran off the stock and left us hiding in the brush fearing for our lives. There was nothing more I could do.'

'So what are you doing here?'

Joey shrugged his narrow shoulders and averted his eyes. 'We're thinking about California. A couple of the horses came wandering back in the next day, looking for some grain, and I roped them. I hope you don't mind. I had to have something for Lupe and the children.'

'No, of course I don't mind,' Auggie said quietly. 'I owe you a month's pay and it doesn't look like I'll be able to pay you.'

'Let me keep the horses and we'll call it even.'

Auggie climbed down from the saddle, arched his back against the strain of riding, and nodded. 'You've got a deal.'

'How long has it been since you've eaten?'

Auggie wagged his head and glanced hopefully at the fire. 'Not since early this morning.'

'Yeah, that's about what I thought. If you're hungry, pull up a rock. We have plenty of rice and beans.'

Joey turned toward the big boulders beside the lower tank and lifted his hand. 'You can come out, Lupe. It's Auggie and he's hungry.'

Auggie grinned when he saw Joey's stocky little wife detach herself from the shadows and amble into the scant circle of light from the fire. Close on her heels was her younger sister, pretty Becky Camacho, the children — twelve-year-old Pepito, little Maria — and Fernando Vargas, a gaunt-faced *vaquero* from Piedras Negras who could never get enough to eat but was one of the better bronc stompers in the crew.

Lupe was grinning happily at the sight of him and didn't slow down until she'd rounded the fire and squashed him to her big bosom in a warm and familiar bear hug. She'd run the kitchen for him back at the ranch ever since they'd started and had always treated him as if he were one of her own children.

'I think I don't see you no more, *patrón*,' she murmured. 'You are well?'

'Yes, I am well. And you?'

'Always the same,' she said softly. She dug an enamel plate from a wicker basket on the ground and started spooning beans on to it from a kettle next to the fire.

He mussed Pepito's hair when he came within reach and got the same playful scuffle he always got from the boy. He turned then and picked tiny Maria up in his arms.

'And how's my best girlfriend?' he asked, planting a kiss on her cheek.

'I'm not your girlfriend,' she giggled. '*Tía* Becky is.'

'Yeah, I know, but it's supposed to be a big secret.'

Becky, too, stepped into his arms for a hug and a kiss on the cheek, but, in keeping with the strict old Mexican customs, it was much more reserved than Lupe's had been.

'I'm happy to see you again, Auggie,' she purred close to his ear. 'We heard they took you to Yuma. You escape from the hoosegow over there?'

His breath caught in his throat as it always did when he looked into those flashing black eyes of hers; there was little doubt in his mind that one day, if everything went well for him, he'd be asking this girl to marry him.

'No, not from the prison,' he said. 'I ran away from that wagon they use to haul prisoners back and forth.'

'And good for you, *hijo*,' Lupe interrupted, handing him the plate. 'Here, you eat now.'

Nando Vargas pushed his wide black sombrero back on his head, grinning sheepishly like a boy caught writing a bad word on the chalkboard at school, and dropped on to a boulder beyond the fire.

'Looks like you ran into a mule shoe while it was still on the mule, *patrón*.'

'Feels like it, too,' Auggie mumbled. 'You all right, Nando?'

'Yeah, but I'd sure like to get another crack at some of Keogh's men.'

'I'll take care of your horse, Uncle Auggie,' little Pepito interrupted, staying carefully out of his reach.

'Thanks, Pepito. Remind me to bring you some candy next time I see you.' Auggie eased himself down to sit on a slab of rock close to the fire and started in on the food.

Becky straightened her skirt behind her and lowered herself to sit beside him. 'Your face is bruised,' she murmured at his shoulder. 'Did they hurt you?'

At five foot six, she was a little taller than most Mexican girls and seemed secretly proud of the extra height. She had wide-set black eyes, a slender nose, lips made for kissing, and her hair always smelled faintly of soap.

She was one of the most level-headed women Auggie had ever met, down to earth, living life according to her own standards, and attractive enough that he'd be proud to have her on his arm strolling around the town plaza on a quiet Sunday afternoon.

34

A man could damned sure do worse.

He never had figured out what Becky saw in him.

He knew his flint-grey eyes seemed out of place in a face burned dark by the desert sun and his dark hair curling over his shirt collar like the tail feathers of an old Shanghai rooster, and he'd been told more than once that he had the angular features of a hawk.

Between that and the livid white bayonet scar on the angle of his jaw, he decided, he must be one scary *hombre* to look at.

All things considered, it was a wonder Becky and the kids hadn't run away in fear at the very sight of him.

The two women had been in charge of the kitchen for him back at the ranch since they'd started and he hadn't had a single complaint from the crew in all that time. Always good food on the table and always plenty of it.

'I'm OK,' he said around a mouthful of beans. 'They kicked me around a little, split my lip, but I got past it. How about you? You didn't get hurt when Keogh's men came down there?'

'No. They didn't see us.'

'Is that Territorial prison as bad as they say, Auggie?' Joey asked from across the fire.

'Worse,' Auggie muttered. 'It sits on the top of a hill right where the Gila River dumps into the Colorado and the walls are eighteen feet high. Hotter than six kinds of hell up there and there's almost no chance of anyone breaking out.'

'Damn!'

Auggie let his eyes sweep over what was left of his little crew and continued almost as though he was thinking out loud.

'Yeah, they've got a guard tower on every corner manned by riflemen twenty-four hours a day and the main tower, up over the water tank, has a Lowell battery gun in it that can fire six hundred rounds a minute.'

'Six hundred rounds a minute!' Joey blurted. 'Are you kidding me?'

Auggie lifted his hands in resignation. 'That's what they told me. Six men to a cell with a bucket for an outhouse and it stunk to bejesus in there. Big sewer roaches running all over the place and talking wasn't allowed after dark.'

'I heard there were women in there,' Becky ventured softly. There was a tinge of suspicion — maybe jealousy — in her voice but Auggie kept his thoughts to himself.

'There were a few,' he said. 'I saw them through the wire fence in their exercise yard a couple of times, but there was absolutely no contact between the men and women. It meant a stretch in the dark cell if you tried.'

'Were they pretty?'

'Not especially. Big-boned and plain. Not the kind you'd take home to meet the family.'

'What about the food?' Lupe asked softly. Auggie grinned at her question. Knowing her, he'd almost been expecting it.

'Not nearly as good as yours,' he

answered, 'and it never changed. Breakfast was beef hash and coffee every day I was there, lunch was onion stew, and dinner was always beef and boiled potatoes. Prisoners took turns doing the cooking, you know, and I think some of those guys could have burned water.'

'No wonder you're so hungry,' Becky purred by his side. She nodded toward the beans on his plate. 'There's more if you want it.'

'I could use some. My stomach thinks my throat's been cut.'

'*Ay, pobrecito,*' Lupe chimed in, holding her hand out for his plate. 'If you'd just find yourself a nice Mexican wife, like I've been telling you, you'd never go hungry again.'

He raised his hands and looked away. 'Nice girls aren't much interested in a bronc peeler who's all busted up inside from riding the snuffy ones, Lupe. And that doesn't leave much choice for a guy like me.'

She arched an appraising eyebrow at

him and cut her eyes almost imperceptibly across at Becky. 'I know one who might be.'

'Lupe!' Becky admonished, pressing her lips tightly together.

'You going back to Ajo, *jefe*?' Joey asked quietly.

Auggie nodded somberly. 'I have to, Joey. Somehow I've got to clear my name.'

'They'll be waiting for you, you know that, don't you?'

'Yeah, I know.'

'Are you so anxious to die, *hijo*?' Lupe asked over the flames.

'No,' he said, 'I'm not anxious to die. Still, it has to be done. I don't much appreciate having my name dragged through the mud, and no one's going to straighten it out for me. That's something I'll have to do myself.'

He leaned his elbows down on his knees, thinking back to how this whole thing had started.

He'd grown up on the ragged edge of poverty, on a two-by-four patch of bottom land deep in the woods of east Tennessee. His father had probably harvested just as many rocks as he did corn and pumpkins — hell, they *all* had — and he'd gone most of his life on a half-empty stomach, not knowing for sure where his next meal was coming from. Hunting squirrel and white-tail deer had always gotten them through until planting time, but it was not a life he'd have wished on his worst enemy.

He'd beat it out of there the minute he was old enough to join the Army, and in those lean, middle days of the war the Confederates weren't too picky about age. If you were big enough to carry a gun and knew how to use it, you were old enough.

He'd gone over the mountains alone and joined a regiment from North Carolina. First thing he knew he was marching north, barefoot and scared in those cold winter rains, and didn't know the first thing about soldiering.

The company had gotten their tails kicked in pretty hard at Antietam, had turned around and marched back to Fredericksburg, and that had been a fight to remember, hunkered down behind the stone walls on Marye's Heights, just to the west of the city.

He didn't know how many times the blue-bellies tried to storm the ridge after the fog had cleared that day, but they'd turned them back every single time.

They'd moved out to Front Royal for the rest of the winter a few days later and, little by little, he'd matured.

He was a man by then, no matter his age, and had seen enough violence and bloodshed to last him a lifetime.

Like all the others, he'd gone home after the war, to that same rocky little patch of land in the high-up hills, but it had proved to be a short stay.

Nothing much had changed around the old place in his absence, except for Sissy being married and gone. The corn crop was just as sparse, the hogs still too skinny to market, and his father as dour as ever.

Two days. That was all it had taken.

The very last thing he wanted in life was to grow old trying to scrape a living on that god-forsaken little farm, and the old man just couldn't understand it.

'A bird in the hand,' he kept saying, but his words had fallen on deaf ears. There wasn't a chance in hell Auggie could have stayed.

He'd ridden out before sunrise the next morning and had never looked back.

He'd drifted down into the flatlands, crossed the Big Muddy, and trailed west into the Indian Nations, just as so many other displaced Confederates were doing, but there was nothing to keep him there. No work and no future.

After poking around for a couple of weeks he'd made his way down into west Texas and fell in with a crew of mustang men working the wild-horse herds on the Staked Plains. It was there he'd met Joey Benitez. It was there he'd learned the trade.

They'd run probably 400 head of

halter-broke mustangs up the Santa Fe trail to Fort Riley, Kansas, and, seeing first hand the profit that could be made from rounding up wild horses, they decided to strike out on their own and had ridden west into Arizona.

The first mustang herd they'd come across had been in the rocky Ajo Valley, at a place with a series of potholes on it, which the Papago Indians called *Moivavi*, or Many Wells.

They'd erected a gate at the mouth of a box canyon, run the herd in, started breaking them, and found themselves suddenly in the business.

There were dozens of small herds within a few hours of Many Wells, but catching them with as few men as they had at the time had been a real job. Very few saddle horses, burdened with 200 pounds or more of man and tack, could keep up with a wild herd for long.

They'd had to work in relays with fresh horses and riders coming in at regular intervals, and the chases had sometimes lasted for days.

It was bone-crunching work; drifting the herds into a box canyon or hastily erected ocotillo corral, culling out the old and infirm, earing them down at a snubbing post while one man rigged a hackamore over their muzzle and another cinched down a saddle.

A rider stepped into the saddle then, told the men to turn them loose, and the fireworks began.

Most of the time the first buck was straight up and down, landing with a jolt, the second to one side or the other. The rider had to anticipate every move the horse was likely to make and be in position before the next buck started.

The wild horses sunfished, twisting into almost impossible shapes, crow-hopped on stiff legs, grunting and squealing, dust rising around them like a fog, and the peeler doing his level best to stay aboard without holding on to the saddle horn.

That, Auggie had learned the hard way, was known as 'grabbing the apple' among bronc busters and was considered the most shameful, disgraceful thing a rider could possibly do.

The *vaqueros* had come in a few at a time, many of them Joey's relatives from the state of Coahuila, in north central Mexico, and he'd taken on the two women to feed them all.

It had taken them months to build the ranch, whipsawing cottonwood and palo verde for lumber, bronc busters working with axe and adze and spoke-shave, fashioning furniture and fences after an already hard day on the hurricane deck of a wild horse.

Each of them, it seemed, had taken pride in the place, knowing they were part of an elite group and pulling themselves up by their own bootstraps. There had been no complaints from any of them, just nods of approval and claps on the back for a job well done.

It had been a time of contentment, of peace, for them; the Copper King had ended it all with his greed.

Auggie hadn't figured he had that coming. None of them had.

A single letter from his mother had caught up with him in Ajo, telling him his father had passed away in his sleep and she was going back to Kentucky to live with her sister. He'd kept the letter folded up in the crown of his hat for several months, using it in the end to start a fire one bitterly cold winter morning on the Coconino Plateau. That had been the end of it.

There'd been no family traditions to carry on, no legacy to uphold, and precious few cherished memories from his childhood.

He'd learned to rely on himself.

The whole problem was that there was also copper on his place. He'd seen the blue-green patches of surface outcroppings many times, and that was what Keogh was after.

The Copper King had scraped off all the rich surface ore on his place, shipped it around the Horn to a smelter in Swansea, Wales, and would have to start digging now to keep it going. If he could get his hands on the surface copper on Auggie's spread it would save him thousands of dollars in expense.

And, to the Copper King, having money was the be-all, end-all meaning of life.

'You will stay here with us tonight,' Lupe informed him from her seat across the fire. 'I will fill your belly with chorizo and beans in the morning and give you some food for the trail. After that it will be in the hands of God.'

'Let's hope he is charitable,' Becky murmured. 'There are many *banditos* traveling the desert these days.'

'*Sí*,' Lupe added with an evil grin, 'and escaped convicts.'

'Of course I'll stay,' Auggie said quietly. 'I never could walk away from your chorizo and beans.'

He paced around the fire to the edge of the lower tank, where Pepito had deposited his gear, retrieved the deputy's bedroll, and spread it in a spot where heat would be reflected by the boulders but nothing could get behind him.

'I'll ride back with you, Auggie,' Joey said from the fire.

'No, your duty is to the family now. You get them on across the desert to California and find a place to settle. I've been told there are some mighty big herds of mustangs running around in that big valley out there and, if I come out of this thing alive, I'll probably be drifting on to California, too.'

'Nando is here,' Joey countered. 'He can take them on into Yuma and they can wait for us there. You're going to need some help with this and I'm just the little boy to help you.'

'You don't have to do this, Joey.'

'Yeah, I do, *jefe*. Those *vaqueros* that died back there were my friends.'

4

Charlie Keogh stood at the dust-streaked window of the mine office, eyes narrowed into mere slits, his teeth clamped hard together, and crumpled the hand-written note from the telegraph office in his fist.

The message it contained had burned painfully into his mind, seeming almost to mock him.

He didn't like to be mocked.

August Kellerman escaped US marshal's custody 20 miles east of Yuma. Armed and mounted. Last seen heading south.

'God damn the man!' Keogh blurted. 'Is there no quit in him?'

'Sorry, Mister Keogh,' his balding clerk mumbled behind him. 'I'm just the messenger.'

'Oh, get the hell out of here,' Keogh growled over his beefy shoulder.

He waited until he heard the office door close behind him, then smoothed out the crumpled note in his fist and read it yet again. It hadn't changed.

He stomped across to the new H.H. Lloyd map nailed to the wall, traced a path east from Yuma with a blunt finger for what he thought would be about twenty miles, stopped, and scanned the area to the south.

He wasn't a navigator by any stretch of the imagination, but then again he didn't have to be.

There was nothing in that direction except for the trail of El Camino del Diablo. That could mean only one thing . . .

The son of a bitch was coming back to Ajo!

He dug a fat Cuban cigar out of his vest pocket, thumb-struck one of the newfangled lucifer matches, exhaled a great cloud of bluish smoke into the quiet of the room, and let the significance of this new knowledge soak in.

Auggie Kellerman was coming back to kill him. For the first time in his life he was truly afraid.

Charlie Keogh wasn't quite sure how to sidestep this one, yet he knew he had to. He was no match for Kellerman on his own. Never had been and never would be.

Somehow, he needed help.

Without a word he crushed the greenish imported stogie in an abalone shell he used as an ashtray on his desk, tugged the brim of his bowler hat a little lower over his eyes, and marched out of the office.

Yes, he needed help, and, with a businessman's cold instinct, he had a rough idea where he might get it.

'Will you be back, Mister Keogh?' the clerk asked as he paced out.

He didn't respond, just stepped through the door into the gathering darkness and ambled down the street to Ajo's only saloon.

It wasn't much of a place — didn't even have a name in reality, just SALOON painted in foot-tall black letters across a rickety false front — but it was crowded for an early Saturday evening. Grubby miners coming off the day shift and teamsters, killing time while their heavy wagons got loaded, stood shoulder to shoulder at the bar and a pall of grayish smoke hung like a shroud against the ceiling.

He took a seat at his usual table against the wall and waited while George Macomber, the bartender, wiped a film of fine grey dust from the tabletop with a bar rag.

'George,' he said in a hushed voice, 'you've been around this area a long time, so maybe you can help me.'

'What's that, Mister Keogh?'

'Well, for instance, if a man wanted to hire a couple of, oh, let's say . . . unsavory . . . characters for a job he needed done and didn't particularly want that information known all over town, whereabouts would he look?'

The bartender cast a quick glance around the shadowed interior of the joint and folded the bar rag over his forearm. 'Your usual, Mister Keogh?'

Keogh pursed his lips and nodded pensively. 'Yeah, I think some good Kentucky sipping whiskey might be just the thing tonight.'

Macomber paced away, returned in a few minutes with a clean glass, a bottle of his best bourbon, and set them carefully down within Keogh's reach.

'Just how unsavory would these characters have to be?'

The Copper King lifted his hands in uncertainty. 'Oh, you know; good with a gun, not opposed to putting a man out of his misery if he needed a little help. That kind of unsavory.'

George nodded his understanding and leaned down a little closer. 'Well, I think a canny man would probably start by asking a knowledgeable bartender who knew enough to keep his mouth shut.'

Keogh met his eyes evenly and spoke

in little more than a whisper. 'Are you a knowledgeable bartender, George?'

George tilted his head and grinned at him. 'I am that. Among other things.'

'And what exactly does that mean?'

'I wasn't always a bartender, Mister Keogh. Far from it.'

'Well?'

The bartender jerked his head almost imperceptibly over his shoulder. 'You see those two gents at the far end of the bar? The ones in the dark gray Stetsons? That's Harry Briscoe and a guy called Santee. They're both known hardcases and wanted for a dozen crimes back in Texas. Friends of mine, believe it or not, and they've been out of work for some time.'

Keogh narrowed his eyes at him. 'Is that a fact?'

'Yes, sir, it is. You want I should send them over?'

'Sure. Why not? They look like they might appreciate some good Kentucky sipping whiskey tonight.'

The bartender ambled back to the

bar, speaking to a few other customers on the way, and Keogh watched in silence as he worked his way down the length of the bar, pouring shots of frontier whiskey and refilling empty glasses with frothy, amber beer.

He spilled a shot of whiskey into his own glass and waited.

George leaned across the bar then, spoke briefly to the men he'd pointed out, and Keogh saw their eyes come up in sudden interest. It was only minutes before they wandered down to his table.

The taller of the two, a bluff-shouldered man with a lantern jaw and ragged blond hair tufting out over the collar of his shirt, folded his arms across his chest and studied him for a long moment.

'George says you wanted to see us.'

'Yes, I did,' Keogh mumbled. 'I'm . . .'

'We know who you are, Mister Keogh. Seen you around town a time or two. I'm Harry Briscoe, from the Big Bend country, and this here's my partner, Santee.'

Keogh nodded at the informal introduction but didn't offer his hand. 'Have a seat, gentlemen. Could I interest you in a drink?'

'Might as well,' Harry replied. 'There's no one in here to dance with.'

They lowered themselves into the empty chairs at the table and suddenly George was there again with a couple more clean shot glasses.

'These are the men I mentioned, Mister Keogh. You can speak plainly with them. It'll go no further.'

'You got something for us?' the man called Santee rasped. He was a tall man in spite of a stoop that took inches from his stature and had the sallow, black-haired look of a Southern gentleman about him. It didn't fit his reputation and Charlie Keogh didn't trust him for a minute.

'I might have,' he said flatly. 'If you're the right sort.'

'Trust me,' Briscoe cut in, tipping a shot of whiskey into his glass. 'We're the right sort.'

Keogh bobbed his head at the statement and leaned slightly toward them across the table. 'There's a man coming here to kill me. He escaped from the US marshal a little earlier today and is on his way here even as we speak.'

'And you want protection?'

'A little more than that,' he said over the rim of his glass. 'I want this guy dead. He's coming across the Camino del Diablo trail. You'd have to find him down there and gun him down when you do. If you're interested, I'm offering two hundred dollars for the job.'

'The Camino del Diablo, hey?' Santee asked. 'That's a damned lot of territory to cover.'

'Not really,' Keogh replied with a toss of his head. 'He's like a dog on a leash down there.'

'What d'ya mean?'

Charlie Keogh didn't like having to explain the obvious. To anyone. It made him uncomfortable, made him question their mentality, and he preferred to be around people he considered his equal. Unfortunately, these two fell far short of that.

'He'll have to go from one water hole to the next, and there just aren't that many of them down there. My best guess is that he'll be at Papago Wells sometime tomorrow afternoon and we're going to be there to meet him. All you have to do is squeeze off a couple of shots when the time comes.'

'You're going along?'

Keogh nodded. 'Wouldn't miss it for the world.'

'Half up front?'

'No,' Keogh said simply. 'I don't work that way. You'll be paid when I'm sure the job's been done.'

He splashed another shot of the raw whiskey into his glass and held his silence while the two hardcases considered his proposition.

'I can live with that,' Santee murmured after a moment. He turned to Briscoe and cocked his head. 'What do you think?'

Briscoe shrugged. 'Sounds easy......
enough to me and two hundred
dollars is a sight of money.'

He leveled his eyes at Keogh then.
'First thing in the morning?'

'Yes, but I'll want you to stay at my
spread tonight. You'll have to share a
bed but it's comfortable and I've got
one of the best cooks in the entire
Territory. You can follow me out there.'

'We got time for another drink before
we leave?' Santee asked, tapping the
empty glass with his finger. 'I've got a
powerful thirst on.'

'Why not?' Keogh muttered, lifting
his hands in indifference. 'Have four or
five for all I care. As long as I know
you'll get the job done.'

Briscoe snorted loudly at his words.
'Oh, we'll get the job done all right.
Making people dead is what we do
best.'

5

The sorrel whickered softly, stamped a hoof, and Auggie Kellerman awoke to an uneasy hush in the warm Arizona night.

The silence was a warning, and he knew it.

Something was out there.

The fire was down to embers and light was scant; still, he sat up rolling his head, trying to work the kinks out of his neck, and glanced at the dark rocks around them.

On a hunch he nudged Joey Benitez from his sleep and started tugging his boots on. 'Wake up, Joey. Someone's coming in.'

'What makes you think so?' his foreman croaked, rubbing his eyes on the heel of his fist.

'The sorrel,' he whispered. 'That horse is turning out to be a pretty damned good watchdog.'

Joey too sat up, peering around at the rocky wash. 'A little early for a social call, ain't it?'

Auggie nodded his agreement in the darkness, not really sure if the slim Mexican vaquero could see it or not. 'My sentiments, exactly. I'm thinking we might ought to edge back away from the fire a little just in case.'

He slid the long-barreled Colt Peacemaker from its holster, eased his way back in among the boulders, and watched as his foreman rolled out of his worn blankets and stepped into his boots.

'Shove the rest of your bedroll under the blankets, Joey, and leave your hat so it looks like they caught us flat-footed. I want to see how this little visit plays out.'

'I'll drink to that.'

'My kind of guy.'

Joey placed his battered hat on the near end of his blankets and moved away from them in a crouch, clutching the sawed-off scattergun loosely in his hands.

All the horses' ears were perked forward now, their nostrils flaring as they peered intently into the darkness of the rock-strewn canyon, just as he was doing.

The proper thing to do when approaching a stranger's camp after dark was to call out and ask permission to come in. The fact that these visitors — whoever they were — hadn't done so had Auggie on edge.

He was still tired after a long day in the saddle, not nearly enough sleep, and in no mood to take chances.

It just wasn't in him.

The unmistakable sound of a boot scraping through coarse sand came to him in the shadows, then the hoarse, apprehensive whispers of men's voices.

'That's got to be the deputy's sorrel, Ernie.'

'I'd say so.'

Auggie moved slowly to his right, sidling quietly through the granite boulders, trying to pick out some movement in the night, but he could see nothing.

'Which one you think is him?'

'Who cares? Kellerman or some others. We'll still pick up the reward no matter how many of 'em we take down.'

'I think that's him on the right. Bigger'n the rest.'

The thunder clap of a rifle shot ripped through the predawn silence that hung over the tanks, and the yellow flame of a muzzle flash only a few yards away blinded Auggie for a moment.

He heard the ratcheting of a saddle rifle's well-oiled lever action, then another shot ripped through the morning stillness.

He stepped out from behind the boulders, the Peacemaker feeling strangely comfortable in his work-hardened hand, and he was mad. All the way through.

'Sons of bitches!' he growled. 'Don't much appreciate getting shot at in my sleep.'

He squeezed off two quick shots at

the spot where the muzzle flash had been and dodged quickly to his left. No telling where this was going to lead.

'God damn it, Ernie,' a voice groaned. 'I'm hit!'

'To hell with this!' came the other voice. 'Let's get out of here!'

Another shot screamed past Auggie's head, whining loudly as it ricocheted off a big granite boulder, then a thunderous roar shattered the night as Joey Benitez cut loose with his shotgun.

'Awww, Jeeesus — '

They heard a body fall in the deep gravel of the wash and the crunch of running footsteps.

Auggie squeezed off two more quick rounds in that direction and the sound of running footsteps faltered to a stop.

Two down.

How many more were out there?

He froze in position for a few minutes, listening for any further sound of bushwhackers, and heard nothing.

'You OK, Joey?' he called after a minute.

'Yeah, I'm all right. You?'

'I'm OK. You think there's any more of them out there?'

'I don't think so,' Joey said. 'I only heard two voices.'

That was all he had heard, too, and it had not surprised him that they'd mentioned his name when they were cat-footing in.

'Grab a torch from the fire and let's see what we've got out here.'

'Joey?' Lupe croaked from the shelter of the rocks by the fire, '*Estás bien?* Are you OK?'

Joey didn't respond to his wife's worrisome question, just gave her an offhand two-fingered salute, held a mesquite branch in the fire until it flared to life, and came back to Auggie's side.

Together they paced down the narrow canyon, knelt among the rocks and held the torch down close to the sprawled bodies.

'Damn, Joey,' Auggie mumbled, 'you just about cut this poor bastard in half.'

'Yeah, well,' his bandy-legged fore-man replied, 'you mess with the bull you get the horn.'

There was no trace of humor in his voice when he spoke, just the reality of life as he knew it; life in the saddle, trying to pry a decent living from the desert for himself and his family.

'You know them?' Auggie asked.

Joey shook his head. 'Never seen 'em before. They're not Keogh's men.'

'Bounty hunters then. Didn't waste much time, did they?'

'No, and there's probably going to be more.'

Only slowly did the normal night sounds of the desert return to the mouth of the wash; a lone coyote howling in the distance before there was any evidence of dawn, the chirping of crickets, the loud buzz of cicadas, burrowing owls adding their two cents' worth to the quail calls, all signaling the start of a new day.

The eastern horizon gradually turned lighter and the heavy grey shadows, indistinct in the darkness, began to take on the shape of rock and mesquite and palo verde.

Auggie sat back on his heels, studying the steep walls of the canyon. It was a perfect place for an ambush and suddenly he didn't feel comfortable.

'I'd better make tracks out of here, Joey. My being around is putting the family in danger, and I don't want to be responsible for that.'

'Stay long enough to eat anyway, *patrón*,' Lupe said, pushing another ocotillo wand into the embers of the fire. 'It will be a long ride for you, among people who want you dead, and there's no telling when you'll eat again.'

He nodded his understanding and pushed himself erect. 'It will have to be fast. Suddenly I have a bad feeling about this place.'

'The coffee's ready whenever you are,' she said easily.

He clapped his foreman on the shoulder and ambled away toward the fire. 'Come on, Joey, let's wet our whistles.'

'On coffee?' Joey asked behind him. 'After that little set-to, I'd like to wet my whistle with a bottle of Who Hit John.'

'Time enough for that later,' Auggie replied. 'Right now we've got to think about getting to Ajo and back in one piece.'

'Are you planning to start over in California, Auggie?' Becky asked from her seat beside the fire.

He spread his hands, but couldn't ignore the significance of her question.

'I don't know. I've met guys who did some placer mining out there and they all say there are thousands of bangtails running loose in the San Joaquin Valley. They say there are some wearing brands that apparently ran away from ranches and even some mules mixed in with the herds.

'They tell me the vaqueros out there ride everywhere they go, that they wouldn't walk if you paid them. They also say there are more and more people coming into the state every day and there's a big market for saddle stock.'

'It sounds as if we could do well out there,' Becky ventured.

'That's what I'm thinking, too, but we'd have to find a spread to work from and round up another crew of bronc-peelers.'

'We could manage it,' Joey chimed in. 'We always have.'

Auggie glanced across at pretty Becky Camacho, wondering yet again if there really was to be any future with her.

He knew that, if he came out of this little foray alive, wild horse herds would not be the only reason he'd want to move on to California.

He knew, too, that he'd been dreaming of settling down with a woman like her, of putting down roots and leaving some kind of a mark on the land. Something more than a line of hoofprints across some sun-baked playa in the middle of nowhere. Something long-lasting, like children and memories. Something that could be spoken of by his descendants a hundred years from now with voices full of pride.

And that, he decided, was the whole trouble with living in the desert . . .

It made a man think.

6

Auggie collected a hatful of plump tornillo beans and patted the sorrel's jaw as she picked them from his hand. 'You saved my bacon last night, girl,' he said quietly. 'It's been a long time since a horse has done that for me.'

The mare stamped a hoof impatiently at him and shook her bridle. He waited until she was finished with the beans, then pulled the picket pin, led her across to the lower tank, and let her drink while he threw the saddle on and tightened the cinch.

'You two will be careful out there, won't you?' Becky asked close behind him.

The voice broke his train of thought and he glanced quickly around over his shoulder. The sorrel, too, lifted her head.

'As careful as we can be,' he said,

watching the silvery droplets of water falling away from the mare's muzzle. 'More than likely, though, we're going to run into some folks who have different ideas about our wellbeing.'

'You know what I mean,' she protested. 'Just don't take chances that you don't have to. I don't want to get prematurely grey from worrying about you.'

'I'll do my best.'

He gazed into those enticing black eyes of hers for a long minute, searching for something meaningful to say, and felt as if he'd come up short.

'I wish I didn't have to go, that I could just stay here with you and the family, but I don't want to live the rest of my life having the name of a murderer and escaped convict hanging around my neck. Nobody's going to straighten it out if I don't.'

He pulled her into his arms for one last hug, stepped up into the saddle, and nudged the mare toward the mouth of the canyon.

At the same time, beside the fire, Joey hugged the children against his chest admonishing them to behave and mind their mother while he was gone, then he stood erect and held his little wife close for several minutes.

They murmured parting words between themselves, but quietly enough that no one else could hear.

Auggie Kellerman didn't want to hear them, anyway. What they had to say was their own affair, and he was ready to ride.

Becky Camacho stood a pace back, gazing at him with hopes and dreams of the future showing painfully in her eyes.

'I will pray for you, Auggie,' she whispered.

'I hope you do,' he replied. 'I'm going to need all the help I can get.'

'Come back to me in one piece.'

'I'll try, little girl,' he murmured. 'I'll really try.'

'See that you do. We were made for each other, you and I, a matched pair, and we both know it. I don't know what

I would do with myself if you were no longer in my life.'

There was nothing more he could say. She'd laid it out on the table without mincing any words and he couldn't argue with the simple truth of it.

'Nando,' Joey muttered when he climbed aboard his little pinto, 'you'll save probably twenty miles by going through the pass and across the Yuma Desert instead of heading north to the Gila.

'When you get to Yuma, look up my uncle Ponce at Bender's Livery Stable. He'll give you a place to stay.'

'Ponce's there?'

'Last I heard he was. He's a good man and has worked hard for what little he has.'

Fernando nodded that he understood and folded his arms across his chest. 'You don't worry about me, *primo*, I'll be respectful and help out any way I can. I met him a long time ago in Piedras Negras, you know.'

'And you take good care of my family,' Joey said firmly. 'I'm depending on you.'

'On my honor,' Vargas uttered.

Joey pushed his dark grey sombrero forward on his head and snugged up the chin strap, even though there was not a breath of wind in the canyon.

'I'm ready when you are, Auggie.'

Auggie lifted his hand in farewell to the women-folk, nodded curtly to Nando Vargas, and touched heels to the mare.

They rode down out of the Tinajas Altas Mountains side by side into a dust-hazy dawn, peering ahead at one of the driest stretches of trail known to mankind: The Devil's Highway.

Hell on a hot day.

The day dawned bright, the valley heavy with the smell of sage and creosote. Birds had been singing for more than an hour, their solos building in a crescendo just before the sun pushed its brassy face above the far hills. Loggerhead shrikes, cactus wrens, tiny grey darters, and the chorus slowly dwindled as the temperature began to rise.

Off in the distance the serrated peaks of the Cabeza Prieta range were still in shadow and Auggie could see no movement in the wide valley below them.

It was a chancy thing, this riding back to Ajo, and he knew it before they started. They were going to be badly outgunned and the odds were long they'd never make it.

Every lawman in the Territory would be after him, trying to make a reputation for himself, and bounty hunters, hungry for a fast buck, would shoot first and ask questions later.

The Quechan trackers would try to take him back alive, of course, because there was always the chance he'd escape again and they'd pull down another fifty dollars in reward money every time they brought him back. Still, he realized that if he gave them any trouble at all it was easier for them just to plug him once and drape his carcass over a horse.

They got paid either way.

And, chancy as it was to go back, he didn't feel as if he had a choice.

He needed no one to tell him this was a desperate land he was riding into. All travel in this part of the Territory was ruled by the need for water, and, no matter what a man's final destination might be, the trails all converged at the water holes.

There was no other way it could be, for without water both man and horse would die.

Tule Tank sat roughly twenty miles to the southeast in a steep rock-filled canyon and, with any luck at all, there'd be enough water left in it to water the horses and let them graze for an hour or so before moving on. He knew the desert bighorn sheep drank there at night and the last time he'd been there he'd seen mountain lion tracks in the sand.

Beyond that the nearest reliable water was at Papago Wells, another thirty miles across deep pink-sand playas and black lava fields from the Pinacate, an alien moonscape of extinct cinder cones and volcanic craters farther to the south in Sonora.

They passed the pitiful collection of thirty-year-old grave markers at the foot of the rocky Tinajas Altas slope but paid them little mind, riding cautiously instead to avoid raising a dust.

A flock of doves hurtled by overhead and Auggie clenched his teeth at the ominous silence that followed. The sounds of the desert dwindled away quickly once the sun came up, all the night-hunters and foragers scurrying back to the shelter of their nests and burrows before the real heat of the day began.

Not so for the two riders at the bottom of the Lechuguilla Valley. For them there was no choice.

It was coming on to be another scorcher and there'd be no shade this side of the tanks.

'You think there's any water left in Tule Tank?' he asked Joey over his shoulder.

'There was when we came through yesterday and I haven't seen any other people on the trail.'

'Thank God for small blessings.'

They were abreast of the distinctive peak of Tordilla Mountain looming just north of the trail when Joey eased the little pinto mare he always rode in close to Auggie's side.

'There's a dust plume behind us. Three or four riders I'd make it out to be and they're coming on fast.'

Auggie nodded ponderingly and twisted in the saddle to stare at the plume once again. 'Yeah,' he said, 'I saw it a few minutes ago. Way too much dust for one man.'

'Bounty hunters?'

'That'd be my guess. Amazing what some men will do for a few bucks.'

'Well, it's a hard life any way you slice it,' his foreman muttered. 'You mind if I ask you what happened that day with Ram Garza, *jefe*?'

He glanced quickly around, but could see no malice or doubt in Joey's look. It was a fair question.

'Not at all,' he said quietly. 'I've got nothing to hide.'

'I'm listening.'

'Well, first off you know Keogh was interested in mining the copper on our place and I had no real claim to it.'

'I didn't know that.'

'Yeah, that Homestead Act the Congress passed way back when was for people who had never borne arms against the Government and, as an ex-confederate soldier, I didn't qualify unless I signed some kind of loyalty oath. I never signed the damned thing — a whole lot of us didn't — so all I had was squatter's rights to the place, and that was shaky at its very best.'

'That's all a lot of people have,' Joey offered.

'Anyway, Keogh had offered to buy me out a couple of times and I turned him down.'

'Yeah, I remember you mentioning that.'

Auggie tugged the brim of his

low-crowned hat a little lower, shielding his eyes against the sun and continued:

'The day this thing with Garza happened, Keogh sent one of his men down asking me to meet with him in his office, you know? I thought he might want to talk about buying me out again so I went.

'When I knocked on the door, he called 'Come in' and then there was a shot. It was *his* voice, Joey. I heard it plain. He was there. Except when I pushed the door open, he wasn't. Only Ramiro Garza lying dead on the floor, and he'd been shot in the back.'

'Damn!'

'The door bumped on something and, when I looked down, I saw it was my gun. *My* gun! How the hell he got it I'll never know, but there it was. Of course I picked it up. Who wouldn't?'

He swallowed against the harsh lump that had formed in his throat at the memory of it and studied Joey's eyes.

'All those teamsters came running in right at that moment and there I was, standing over a dead body with a still-smoking gun in my hand. What else could they think?'

'What a set-up,' Joey droned. 'Sounds like Keogh played you like a trout.'

'That's the way I saw it, too. They tied me up, hauled me to Tucson and the judge sentenced me to be hung. As pretty a frame job as you've ever seen, but it was Keogh killed him. I know it and Keogh knows it, and somehow I've got to prove it.'

'How'd you end up in Yuma?'

'I'm damned if I know,' Auggie said with a shrug. 'Maybe they expected a lynch mob or something and didn't trust their own jail. All I know is I was in the back of that tumbleweed wagon all that afternoon and they slapped me around pretty good when I got there.'

The sorrel drew up suddenly then, her ears perked forward and she turned sideways to the trail, somehow reluctant to go on. Auggie narrowed his eyes at her reaction and slid the heavy Colt Peacemaker out of its holster.

Something was seriously wrong here and the sorrel had sensed it.

Even for a horse he'd known less than two days, that was almighty strange behavior and he was instantly alert.

He heard the sudden crack of a rifle shot, saw the puff of smoke from behind a clump of prickly pear cactus, and felt the jolt as it tore away the horn of his saddle. The mare buck-jumped to the side, wild-eyed and snorting loudly.

A pair of Indians stood up in the brush then, wearing nothing but un-bleached cotton pants and leveling the rifle for another shot.

'Apaches!' Joey shouted, swinging his shotgun up.

'No,' Auggie called, tugging the mare's head around. 'They're Quechan trackers and I've been expecting them.'

Auggie touched heels to the sorrel's flanks and she leaped toward the ambushers as if she'd been doing it all her life.

He was starting to like this horse.

He swung down on the sorrel's off side, pony express style, charging into the Quechans at a full gallop and firing under her neck.

Apparently the Indians had never seen such a move before and Auggie wasn't sure if it was surprise or admiration on their faces. Either way they lowered the rifle and simply stood there, like targets in a shooting gallery, watching him come in.

He saw blood erupt from the chest of the nearer warrior. The other spun on his heel, sprinting toward an outcropping of black lava rock, and Auggie put one through his ear. The warrior pitched headlong into the rocks and was still.

The sorrel slid to a halt, nostrils distended, and Auggie felt the sudden rage that had come upon him fall away.

'God damn it,' he bellowed. 'It didn't have to be this way.'

'No time to stew about it now, *jefe*,' Joey said, reining in beside him. 'That dust plume back there is getting close, and I think we'd better get to Tule Tank before those gents do. If they turn out to be unfriendly, we're going to be in trouble.'

Joey was right, of course. Whoever was kicking up that dust back there was coming on strong and it was no laughing matter.

He met Joey's eyes and nodded. 'Let's ride.'

7

Charlie Keogh leveled his eyes at Asa Hodges as he swung up into the saddle. 'Everything ready?'

'I think so,' the hostler mumbled. 'Plenty of food and water. Plenty of ammunition.'

'All right, then, let's get it done.' Keogh made an exaggerated sweeping gesture with his hand toward the south and the hint of a smirk spread across his thin lips. 'After you, sir.'

He touched spurs to the big zebra dun he customarily rode and glanced around at the others — as unlikely a bunch as he'd ever ridden with — trailing out in some sort of understood pecking order.

Asa Hodges, the only one of them who really knew the desert, took the lead, of course, then came himself. Behind him the two gun hands he'd hired last night slouched along, doing their level best to seem aloof, but tolerating the ride because the pay was good.

Bringing up the rear were two more of his hired hands; Buck Renner, an old-time plainsman who did what he was told but couldn't think past payday, and Paddy Logan, an Irish kid from the streets of New York who'd come West on one of the orphan trains and run away from his foster parents the very first chance he got.

It was all the kid could do to sit a full-grown horse, yet he considered himself some kind of rough-and-tumble trail hand. He'd recently taken to carrying a gun and Charlie Keogh had no idea what was in his mind. Nor did he care, as long as the kid did as he was told.

Once they were away from his big hacienda, Keogh settled back in the saddle and scanned the desert close around them with a jaundiced eye.

Rock and cactus. Cactus and rock. It

was always the same and it was beyond him how some people could stand to live in such a place.

His thoughts drifted to San Francisco, the tang of the salt sea air, the elegant theaters, the late-night parties in the drawing rooms of the upper crust, and he smiled at the memories.

Yes, sir, that was the place for him.

He'd spent a year up there when he first came West, right at the time the Comstock Lode was really being developed, and had witnessed first hand some of the fancy didoes being cut by the heavy investors in buying shares in it on the San Francisco Stock Exchange. He knew many of them personally: John Mackay, Jim Flood, Eilley Orrum Bowers.

As a matter of fact, it was John Mackay who had steered him toward the copper in Arizona, and he'd studied the basics of mining it up in the Morenci district.

Using the tactics he'd learned in San Francisco, it hadn't taken him long at all to gain control of the mining in Ajo and he'd been on Easy Street ever since.

It was time now to just sit back and enjoy the ride.

And, once this little episode with Auggie Kellerman was over, that was exactly what he intended to do.

He could put the mining operation in the hands of a competent manager, pay him a reasonable salary for his efforts, and he himself could just sit back and relax in the luxury of a swank hotel.

Was that too much to ask?

They trailed past Darby Well just after the sun shoved its glaring face above the hills east of the Ajo Valley and through Growler Pass by mid-morning. Ahead of them then was a stretch of flat, monotonous desert studded with clunks of black lava rock and organ pipe cactus as far as the eye could see.

He wagged his head grimly, hoping none of the others would see his disgust, but it was there, in him, and he knew it.

No, the desert was not for him. The emptiness, the savagery of it left a bitter taste in his mouth. It was a place for commoners, for brutes, and he didn't consider himself common.

Ten yards behind him, and without his knowledge, Harry Briscoe and the dark-haired Santee eyed his broad back.

'You know,' Briscoe said in a hoarse whisper, 'this could be a real sweet deal for us.'

'How so?'

'Well, we've already seen Keogh's set-up back in town. Except for a couple of Mexican servants, his entire crew is out here.'

'And?'

'And he said all we had to do was squeeze off a couple of shots when the time comes. I'm thinking we might squeeze off a couple of extra shots and have his whole spread in our hands.'

Santee bobbed his head and grinned. 'Don't sound that hard to me.'

'I know he's carrying gold in his vest pocket,' Briscoe murmured. 'Heard it clinking around in there, and more'n likely there's some in the saddle bag. On top of that, I'd be real surprised if he didn't have a stash of it hidden somewhere in the hacienda. Could be a real big haul for us.'

Santee didn't respond for a long moment, then nodded in assent. 'I'm for it. Probably be enough to finance us all the way into northern California and there's supposed to be some rich pickings out there.'

'That's what I'm thinking, too. Them stinking Texas Rangers got no authority whatever out there.'

'Just let me know when you want to open the ball. I got no use for two-bit toffs like this guy.'

Harry Briscoe chortled half under his breath. 'That makes it unanimous then. I got no use for the sawed-off little runt, either.'

He glanced over his shoulder at the two Keogh hirelings riding behind them, and continued quietly:

'I'm pretty sure I could figure out a

use for some of his money — a new pair of boots, a new saddle — but these East Coast blowhards just tend to rub me the wrong way.'

Santee bobbed his head again. 'Like I said, just let me know when you want to open the ball.'

★　★　★

They rode into the narrow Tule Tank Canyon with their guns drawn, half-expecting another ambush, but the water-worn rocks held no surprises for them.

Auggie swung down from the saddle at the edge of the lower tank, leaving Joey to water the horses in the dark pools while he paced back along the defile and hunkered down in the boulders where he could watch the trail behind them without skylining himself.

He squinted at a small dust devil that had kicked up half a mile away; it meandered through the sage and creosote bushes for a hundred yards, then petered out. Below him, on the flats, a quail called. There was no other sound.

The dust plume was only about quarter of a mile out when his foreman crouched down beside him.

'More Quechans?'

'No,' Auggie replied, wagging his head. 'An Indian would never allow that much dust. These are strictly greenhorns.'

'I staked the horses in a patch of galleta grass up there,' Joey said. 'Give them a chance to graze a little before we move on.'

'You think we should chance a fire?'

'I'd wait until we see what these jaspers are all about.' Joey nodded toward the bottom of the arroyo just as the riders came into sight.

There were four of them, riding single file, and they were studying the tracks on the ground rather than trying to pick out riflemen hidden in the rocks, as they should have been doing.

One day, Auggie knew, their carelessness would get them killed.

And it could very easily be today.

'That's far enough,' he called from the rocks. 'Who are you?'

They drew up in the shade of the rare elephant tree growing at the mouth of the canyon and, for the first time, had sense enough to glance around at their surroundings.

'Take it easy, mister,' the heavy-shouldered man in front called back. 'We're peaceable.'

'Depends on which end of the firearm you're looking at, doesn't it?'

'Sounds about right to me.'

'You haven't answered my question,' Auggie called again. 'Who are you?'

The heavy-shouldered man swiveled his head, scanning the three behind him for a brief moment, then turned back to the seemingly empty canyon ahead of him.

'Drifters,' he said loudly. 'Heading east.'

'Yeah? Well, I don't think so. I think you're bounty hunters trailing August Kellerman.'

'And why would you go thinking a thing like that?'

'Because I'm August Kellerman and you've been dogging my tracks for a couple of hours.'

The heavy-shouldered one went for his gun without speaking and Auggie drilled him.

The shot snapped him backwards out of the saddle as if he were a rag doll. The strawberry roan he'd been riding charged straight ahead, up the canyon, toward the irresistible smell of water.

The other three men in the ragged line piled off their mounts, diving into the rocks for cover, and, for a few moments, there was a welcome quiet in the arroyo.

'You're outgunned, Kellerman,' one of the three called.

'And you're out of water.'

He felt the perspiration trickle down his back under the shirt and fed a new bullet into the Peacemaker's cylinder.

'You can ride out if you want to,' he called after several minutes. 'I won't shoot and nobody else needs to get hurt.'

'We need water.'

'Heart Tank is about twelve miles northeast of here and there may be some water in it. You can try for that.'

A bullet whined off the rock just inches from his head, splattering chips of granite in his face, and he scooted several feet to his left for better cover.

He glanced across at Joey Benitez, hunkered down beside a massive granite boulder, but didn't speak. There was not a breath of wind in the canyon and the sun beat down unmercifully from a brassy, cloudless sky.

He studied the rocks and cholla below him, watching for some kind of movement, but there was nothing. Then he saw a slight discoloration in the desert floor — tan instead of grey — and he watched it for several minutes through sweat-blurred eyes.

It was a boot. A cowhide boot. And it was enough for him.

He steadied the Peacemaker on the

heel of his hand, exhaled slowly, and squeezed off his shot.

The heel of the boot flipped crazily through the air, and the man wearing it — whoever he was — yelped like a little girl.

He stood up, an insane glare twisting his face, and plodded up the canyon towards them with a sixgun in each hand. His shots were wild, random, and it was painfully obvious that he had no idea in the world what he was firing at.

Still, he was firing and that made him dangerous.

Auggie leveled the Peacemaker yet again and shot him between the eyes. He crumpled in a patch of jumping cholla as his pistol went off yet again into the gravel of the wash.

'We're coming out, Kellerman,' one of the other men shouted. 'You said you wouldn't shoot.'

'I won't shoot,' he called, 'as long as you're above board about it, but if I see you two on the trail again I'm going to come helling.'

'You won't see us again. We're going to cut and run for Yuma Crossing.'

'Good plan.'

'We're coming out now,' the man yelled.

The two of them stood up then, disheveled and dusty, and Auggie stood, too, meeting their looks without flinching.

They paced away toward their horses, talking quietly between themselves.

The thing was, their guns were still unshucked, dangling almost casually in their hands, and a less vigilant man might not have noticed.

Not so with Auggie Kellerman. He *did* notice.

A trusting soul he was not.

Never had been.

The two men swung up into their saddles without a word, tugged their horses' heads around, and started firing.

He felt a bullet pluck at his sleeve, another took the hat off his head, and he started fanning the Peacemaker at them as fast as he could pull the trigger.

For the second time that day a deafening roar shattered the desert air as Joey Benitez unloaded both barrels of his shotgun at the pair and, just that suddenly, the shooting ended.

The horses danced away toward the safety of the flats and they didn't bother trying to stop them. It was enough just to be alive.

They stood in stunned silence for a long minute, gazing at the four bodies sprawled around the foot of Tule Tank Canyon. It made no sense.

'Like you said,' Joey muttered, 'strictly greenhorns.'

'And not very good at it, either.'

8

The Copper King's caravan of misfits trailed through Cholla Pass before noon and ambled slowly down into Cinnamon Flat without talking.

The sun beat down on their shoulders from an unforgiving sky, stifling, relentless, and there was no shade to be had. Heat waves shimmered in the distance, distorting Keogh's view of the desert around them and he clenched his teeth in dismay.

It was impossible to believe anything could live out here, yet he could see their traces everywhere he looked. Coyote tracks crossed the fine brown dust in front of him, kangaroo rat holes were there under the bushes, rabbit droppings scattered around, the drag marks of a heavy lizard lay in the sand, and overhead, the small black curves of turkey vultures spiraled up on rising currents of air.

He glanced around at the rest of the group, lost in his own misgivings, wondering if any one of them had the common sense God gave a doughnut.

It was all too much for Charlie Keogh and he was starting to regret his decision to come along. There had to be better things for him to do.

Strangely enough, he was thinking about his family.

Although they hadn't been members of the Society of Friends, his family had a small farm just outside the predominately Quaker community of London Grove, Pennsylvania, and he'd grown up seeing their somber clothing and hearing the incessant thees and thous in their speech.

That was also where he'd met Jennifer Hayes.

She'd been visiting friends for the summer, a remarkably beautiful girl, and she'd fascinated him with her big-city ways, her big-city talk.

Somehow his mother had known

from the very beginning that Jenny wasn't the woman he thought she was and tried everything she knew to make him understand it, too. When all her efforts failed, she had simply cut the apron strings and let Charlie be responsible for his own decisions.

And, while it had never been said in so many words, it was always understood that he'd have to live with the consequences of his decisions. Good, bad, or indifferent.

He'd spent the first few years of his adult life playing the devoted husband to Jenny, except he had never felt the devotion.

He'd gotten married and had a child because it was the accepted thing to do, but the entire experience had drained him.

All give and no take.

It had grated against everything he believed in, and there was no way he could renege on it. Not and hold his head up in polite society.

When she'd taken their daughter and

gone back to Baltimore to live with her family, it had felt almost like a reprieve. It was only later, when she succumbed to influenza, that he felt any remorse at all.

And even that hadn't lasted very long.

He was already in the West by then and there was little connection left with his family. He made no effort to rekindle any kind of relationship with his daughter, figuring she would be better off without him in her life and, for sure, she had no place in his.

It was too late now to even consider it.

He shook his head, forcing himself back to the reality of the moment, forcing himself to analyze this problem he had with Auggie Kellerman in a rational, businesslike manner.

Kellerman was the one person in the world who knew the truth in all this, the one man who could bring his copper empire crashing down around his ears.

Keogh knew full well there was only one person at the mine who might have seen him ride in and out that day.

Skinny Gil Torres, the lookout.

He'd been on watch on the rooftop that day, keeping an eye peeled for Apache warriors even though Ajo was a little far west for them, and, if he hadn't fallen asleep on the job up there, as he usually did, he might possibly have seen him.

If Kellerman could get to Torres and make him testify before one of the Territorial judges, the Copper King's game was virtually over.

His reputation, his very name, would be dragged through the mud, and odds were short he'd end up on the business end of a hangman's noose himself.

And, no matter what else came to pass, he couldn't allow that to happen.

No matter what else happened out here, Auggie Kellerman had to die.

It was the only way.

Irritably he dug his spurs into the flank of the zebra dun and loped up next to Asa Hodges.

'How much farther, Hodges?' he demanded loudly.

'Not far,' the old-timer replied. He stabbed a finger at the hazy horizon ahead of them. 'That's the Agua Dulce range right there. Papago Wells are in the foothills at the far end of the range.'

'And what's down that way?' Keogh asked, jerking his head toward the south.

'Nothing good, you can bet on that,' Hodges droned. 'The Pinacate Desert, they call it. I've never been in there, you know, but I heard some old Papago Indians talking about it once.

'To them it's sacred ground, where the cave of I'toi, their greatest god, is located, but the reality of it is it's the most desolate stretch of country on God's green earth. Lava beds, volcanic craters, twisted rocks, scorpions, and snakes. The whole damned place was named after a Mexican stinkbug. That ought to tell you something.'

'No need for us to go down there?'

Keogh mumbled.

'No, we'll be at the Wells in about two hours.'

He lapsed into silence then, again forcing himself to analyze the situation in a businesslike manner.

That there would be gunplay at Papago Wells was a foregone conclusion. If Auggie Kellerman was to die out here, there was nothing else for it. The question that bothered him was whether or not he had to be a part of it.

He was a man who appreciated safety and comfort and, with his money, it seemed reasonable that he could afford some.

He had no intention of sticking his neck out this late in the game. Not for the likes of Harry Briscoe and that sallow Santee character he rode with.

They weren't his friends by any stretch of the imagination. Nor did he want them to be. They were hired hands, nothing more, nothing less, and they could be replaced in a heartbeat.

They were, after all, the big-name gunfighters, the quick draws, the dead shots. They'd faced down men before and by now it should be almost second nature to them.

Like breathing.

If they survived another shoot-out, then good on them.

If they didn't . . . well . . . so much for living legends.

He had his own future to think about, for Christ's sake. The wealth, the comfort, San Francisco in the fall. Everything he'd worked for. And not one little bit of it depended on his chipping in on a pitched gun battle in the Agua Dulce Mountains.

'Is there a back way out of the Wells, Hodges?' he asked over his shoulder.

Hodges met his look evenly and the challenge in his eyes was obvious. He didn't put it into words, of course, but it was there.

And Keogh saw it.

'Sure,' Hodges said flatly. 'There's always a back way out.'

* * *

Joey Benitez slouched back against the trunk of an ironwood tree, legs splayed out at a comfortable angle, and a pensive look spreading across his face.

'I'm too old for this kind of nonsense,' he muttered. 'Men I don't know trying to kill me, a tiny fire in the middle of nowhere, nothing to drink but scalding black coffee, and my only companion a plug ugly gringo like you.'

'You didn't have to come.'

'Sure, I did,' he answered. 'We've come a far piece, you and I. From the Llano Estacado to the Mojave Desert and back, living by the rope and the gun, getting by the only way we knew how. Who the hell else was going to cover your backside if it wasn't me?'

Auggie lowered his gaze to the smokeless iron-wood fire and pondered the foreman's words.

They were true and he knew it.

Joey and Lupe, little Becky Camacho, the vaqueros they'd ridden with . . . they were the only family he had, the only ones who gave a good goddamn whether he lived or died, and he had no idea what he'd do without them.

They'd been there with him through thick and thin, sharing what came of luck and what came of skill. The good and the bad together. They were more like family to him than his own blood kin had ever been.

'Who the hell else would put up with me?' he countered.

He held the smoke-blackened coffee pot out, nodding toward Joey's cup, and filled it to the brim when the scrappy foreman held it out.

'What you said back there at Tinajas Altas about starting over in California,' Joey ventured. 'Were you serious about that?'

'There's no guarantee we're going to walk away from this mess, Joey, but if we do, yeah, I'm dead serious about it. I don't know any other way to make a living.'

Joey nodded his agreement. 'That's

what I thought you'd say.'

'What makes you ask?'

The foreman took a long swig of his coffee, apparently considering such a move, before he spoke again.

'I've got some shirt-tail relatives living out there, Auggie. They got part of an old Spanish land grant near the Mission San Juan Bautista and wrote that they'd be happy to put us up for a while.'

'When was that?'

'Quite a while back . . . before all this trouble with Keogh started . . . but I'm thinking we could hole up there till we got on our feet. It's a shot.'

Auggie narrowed his eyes, pondering the idea. 'Where is this Mission San Juan Bautista?'

'Somewhere north of Monterey. Not too far from the coast as I understood it and about a day's ride to San Francisco.'

'That'd be the big market, right there.'

'That's what I'm thinking, too,' Joey

said quietly. 'They say the place is covered with live oak trees, has a lot of pasture on it, and there's supposed to be a pass just east of them over into that big valley you were talking about.'

Auggie took a sip of his own coffee, rinsing the dust out of his mouth. 'Sounds like a possibility.'

'Possibility?' Joey huffed. 'It sounds like a goddamned running start to me!'

'We couldn't stay there forever.'

'No, we'd have to find our own spread after a while, but it would give us a chance to look around first. Find us a place with water and forage, timber for building. We might even be able to run a few head of cattle.'

Auggie winced at the idea. 'I don't know the first thing about running cattle.'

'What's to know? You turn them out to graze and they get meat on their bones.'

'What about the relatives?' Auggie asked quietly. 'They might not cotton to the idea of having some gringo bronc-buster hanging around.'

'Now that dog won't hunt. You're going to end up marrying Becky, and that'll make you family. You'd be as welcome as any of us.'

'You think so?'

'Oh, for Christ's sake, Auggie. Everyone knows that, even Becky. You two have been moon-eyed over each other since you first met. We're all just waiting for you to quit dilly-dallying around and jump the broom.'

'You really think she'd have me, Joey?'

Joey's frown slipped into a wide smile at his question. 'I swear, you're getting a little weak north of the ears. She's waiting, too.'

Auggie swirled the hot coffee around in his cup for a brief moment without responding, gazed away at what he could see of the old Camino del Diablo trail, and resigned himself to the fact that it was time to move on.

He'd already swapped saddles with the one on the bounty hunter's roan, wanting one that still had its saddle horn intact. It also had a new model Winchester saddle rifle riding in a boot.

Massive cumulus clouds were beginning to boil up over the mountains to the east, signaling a shift in the weather pattern that pulled moist air up from the Gulf of Mexico and generated the short-lived thunderstorms of the summer monsoon. He noted with silent apprehension that the wind was picking up.

'You ready to ride, Joey?' he asked quietly.

'Might as well be,' the slender vaquero answered. 'We ain't making any money sitting here.'

'You think there's any more of them out there?'

'Only one way to find out.'

His foreman sloshed the dregs of the coffee on to their small fire and pushed himself up to his full height. 'Let's ride.'

Auggie, too, pushed himself erect, dumped what was left of his coffee into the fire and scraped sand over it with his boot.

Without a word he shoved the dented tin cup into a pocket of the saddle-bag, swung into the saddle, and tugged the sorrel's head around.

'I almost feel sorry for these jokers,' Joey muttered as they rode past the bodies of the four bounty hunters at the foot of the canyon. 'Maybe we should cover them up with rocks to keep the coyotes and vultures away.'

'To hell with them,' Auggie rasped. 'They rode into this with their eyes wide open and they paid the price.'

He heeled the mare into an easy canter, rode out of the sandy wash into a dense thicket of creosote and catclaw, and turned east into the low-lying ridges of Gravestone Pass.

Ahead of them the desert stretched away in an almost unbroken plain of mesquite, towering saguaro cactus, and rock. It was going to be a long afternoon.

'What do you think we'll run into in Ajo, Auggie?'

Auggie wagged his head somberly and

tried to keep the worry out of his voice.

'Trouble with a capital 'T', my friend. Keogh has to know I'm coming by now and it only makes sense that he'll have some kind of a welcoming committee all lined up to meet me when I ride in.

'We can figure they'll have us in a crossfire, probably from rooftops and windows, and they'll have every entrance covered.'

'It sounds like we've got about as much chance as a one-legged man in an ass kicking contest.'

'Just about,' Auggie chuckled. 'What we have to do is try to out-think him.'

'And that may take some doing, *jefe*. From what I've heard, Keogh's got a mind like a bear trap.'

'I've heard that, too. The trouble with bear traps, though, is that just about anything can set them off. It doesn't have to be a bear.'

Joey tilted his head, considering this. 'Funny how everyone thinks he's such a stand-up guy.'

Auggie pulled his hat brim slightly lower and grimaced at the thought. He knew it was true, but there was another part of Keogh's reputation he had heard of, too: that of riding roughshod over people to get things his own way. Not caring one way or the other who got hurt as long as he came out on top.

They were rumors mostly, but in this untamed country it was common knowledge that even rumors generally had their basis in some scrap of truth.

It was not a comforting thought.

He was riding easily, slouched back in the saddle with the bounty hunter's Winchester cradled in the crook of his elbow, Apache style, when the mare's ears perked forward again. She didn't slow her pace any, though, and Auggie thought nothing of it.

Suddenly, only a few yards ahead of them, two riders eased out into the trail, one on either side.

It was big Jim Melnick and Ira Davis, and he knew trouble had found him again.

They were both wearing regular clothes, both forking different horses, and a sardonic grin was quirking Melnick's lips.

'Well, will you look at this, Ira?' he rumbled. 'It's August Kellerman, just like we figured.'

He lifted his gaze to Auggie and narrowed his eyes.

'We saw the bodies up at the High Tanks, Kellerman, and the two dead Indians on the trail back there. That was some damned good shooting, by the way. A running target and you got him right through the head.'

'I never killed a man who didn't have it coming,' Auggie answered.

'Yeah, well, no matter. They're just as dead, ain't they?'

'Friends of yours, Auggie?' Joey asked quietly.

'Not so's you'd notice. They were in the tumble-weed wagon with me and I turned them loose.'

He turned to Melnick, lowering the

Winchester almost imperceptibly towards his midsection. 'I thought you boys were headed north.'

'Just long enough to find some settlers we could talk out of some clothes and horses and guns,' Melnick mumbled. 'We heard the shooting back there at Tule Tank and thought you might possibly need some help.'

Auggie huffed at his statement. 'I seriously doubt you rode all the way down here to see if I needed help.'

'You shouldn't have turned us out like that, Kellerman. It wasn't a very neighborly thing to do, sending us off on some stupid draft horses, not a gun to our names, and still wearing stripes. I told you we wouldn't forget.'

'There wasn't enough to go around any way you sliced it and I had problems of my own right about then.'

Ira Davis nodded toward Joey and chimed into the conversation. 'This the little bastard who likes to cut people down with a shotgun?'

'As a matter of fact, it is,' the

hard-barked foreman replied. 'And the little bastard's name is Joey Benitez.'

Without another word, he emptied both barrels of the scattergun into Davis's belly and didn't bat an eye as the half-breed bandit was swept backwards off his horse.

At that same instant big Jim Melnick whipped an old Colt Army from a worn holster on his hip and fired point blank at Auggie.

Incredibly the shot missed, tearing the sweat-stained hat off his head instead and fanning his face with a breath of dry air as it screamed past.

Almost as a reflex action, Auggie thumbed back the saddle rifle's hammer and squeezed off a reply.

Blood burst forward from the center of Melnick's chest and the lineback dun he straddled suddenly reared up on his hind legs.

The bulky outlaw was dumped unceremoniously off to the side as the horse charged away into the sage with Melnick's foot hung in the stirrup, his body bouncing crazily across the flats.

Auggie levered a new round into the rifle's chamber and watched them go in silence.

'I swear, Auggie,' his foreman droned at his side, 'half the damned country must be gunning for you.'

Auggie didn't respond. Instead he stepped down from the saddle, picked the deputy's hat off a clump of teddy-bear cholla, and held it up to the sun.

'Yeah, but I wish to hell they'd take it easy on this hat. It's the only one I've got and there's not many general stores out this way.'

Joey wagged his head and grinned.

'I don't know about you, Auggie,' he said dubiously. 'I seriously don't know about you.'

9

The Copper King pulled up in the ironwood thicket at the foot of the arroyo, scanning the rocky slopes around him for decent ambush sites.

It was a chance to stack the deck against Auggie Kellerman, and he intended to take it.

'Renner,' he said flatly, cutting his eyes across to the old-time plainsman, 'I want you to hole up in the trees over there, keep your horse out of sight, and don't do any shooting unless Kellerman tries to ride back out of the canyon once he's past you.'

He twisted in the saddle, leveling his gaze at young Paddy Logan, and cleared his throat.

'Are you any good with a rifle?'

'Yes, sir, I am,' the boy answered with a self-conscious grin.

'I seriously doubt that,' Keogh

grumbled, 'but you're all I've got.'

He stabbed a blunt finger at the slope and waited until Logan followed it with his eyes.

'You see that big bluish-colored rock up there?'

'Yes, sir.'

'All right, then. I want you to climb up to that rock, stay out of sight, and keep your eyes open, you understand? What I said to Mister Renner goes for you, too. You don't do any shooting unless Kellerman tries to ride back out once he's past you.'

'Nothing to worry about, Mister Keogh.'

'How I wish I could believe that. You ever kill a man?'

Paddy lowered his eyes at the question, turning suddenly red about the ears. 'No, sir, I haven't.'

'Damn!' Harry Briscoe blurted. 'What a mollycoddle life you must have had. I killed my first man when I was twelve.'

There was nothing Keogh could say to the gunman's boast. He wagged his head doubtfully and pointed on up the canyon with his chin. 'Let's go.'

He touched spurs to the dun's flanks and followed Asa Hodges into the wash.

Papago Wells was a stark and silent place; its three dark pools of water sheltered from the sun by tall, smooth ramparts of bluish lava rock and there was sign on the ground of many, many campfires having burned there.

Below the lowest tank was another dense stand of ironwood and galleta grass, and it was there that the Copper King climbed down from the dun.

He handed the reins over to Asa Hodges and lowered himself to sit on a slab of rock close to the pool. A rock wren trilled loudly from the top of a boulder near him, then flicked away to its nest before the sun sank beyond the high rim of the arroyo.

'First of all,' Keogh rumbled, 'let's get a pot of coffee and something to eat going, then I want a lookout somewhere up there in the rocks, either Briscoe or Santee. Hodges, you stay close to me, and keep your rifle handy.

'We're not dealing with some two-bit cow puncher here. I've got a feeling this guy Kellerman has seen the elephant a time or two and I don't trust him for a Mexican minute.'

'I'll get the fire and the coffee on,' Hodges said with a toss of his graying head. 'Call you boys when it's ready. Bacon and beans will take a while.'

Keogh waited until the two hired guns were out of hearing then fixed his gaze on his aging hostler. 'You said there was a back way out of here?'

Hodges nodded ponderously, piling ironwood twigs in a circle of smoke-blackened rock. 'Right through that cut there, Mister Keogh,' he mumbled, nodding toward a notch in the boulders. 'It's a little brushy but it'll bring you out back down on the flats. You figure we'll have to light a shuck out of here?'

'That's why I want you to stay close to me. If everything goes right, this should be a turkey shoot.'

'Except this turkey can shoot back.'

Keogh narrowed his eyes at the man and there was no hiding the venom in his voice. 'Don't cross me, old-timer. I don't take kindly to being crossed.'

'And I don't take kindly to being double-crossed,' Hodges rasped back at him. 'Looks to me like the only person you're worried about out here is you. I doubt if those two gunslingers in the rocks up there would take kindly to being left behind, either. Maybe I should let them in on your secret plan.'

'They're being well paid. So are you, for that matter.'

'Yeah, and I'd like to live long enough to spend some of it.'

'Stick with me and you will. I don't plan on getting myself shot up out here.'

Hodges rolled his eyes up to an unseen heaven. 'This guy you're hunting may have some different ideas about that.'

'He doesn't even know we're out here.'

'You think he doesn't know we're out here?' the old hostler droned, stirring the kettle of beans. 'Personally, I've got my doubts. You said yourself he wasn't some two-bit cow puncher and you thought maybe he'd seen the elephant a time or two. In my book that makes him a force to be reckoned with.'

Now it was the Copper King's turn to roll his eyes. 'You're giving him a lot more credit than he has coming, Hodges. He's just a simple bronc buster, after all.'

'Yeah? Well, you can call it any way you see it, but the odds are long he knows exactly where you're sitting right this minute, how many guns he's up against, and what our horses had for lunch. It's called savvy.'

He set the lid of the Dutch oven back on the blackened kettle then and continued: 'You may be a big shot businessman, Mister Keogh, but you sure ain't any judge of men.'

'What do you mean by that?'

'Well, think about it. You post a no

account kid up in the rocks and a washed-up plainsman in the iron-wood thicket as bushwhackers and hire two gunhands who're just riding on their reputations. That doesn't say much for your smarts.'

'You know Briscoe and Santee?'

'I've heard of them. Who hasn't?'

* * *

Auggie felt the first fat raindrops from the thunder-storm patter on his shirt as they rode out of a wide basin of reddish-colored silt spread across the desert floor. He glanced uneasily at the ridges of razor sharp lava stretched out ahead of them and grimaced.

This was only the beginning.

They rode a hundred yards off the main trail, through the thick mesquite and creosote bushes, using an old Apache dodge to keep from being seen, and rode slowly enough to avoid raising a dust.

Even at that, he knew their situation was shaky.

He was well aware that, from the sheer high rocks behind the main tank at Papago Wells, a rider could be seen several miles out.

Anyone watching from up there would definitely have the drop on them, and there was no way they could avoid going in.

Cipriano Well was still too far away, as was Gunsight, and they had to have water for the horses.

'I don't like the looks of this, Joey,' he said, peering ahead at the Agua Dulce Mountains. 'It's too quiet, too pat.'

'I'm with you on that one. If anyone's in there, it seems like we should be seeing some sign of them. A smoke or something. I haven't even seen a bird on the wing for half an hour and they're usually the first sign of trouble.'

Auggie nodded his agreement and stepped down from the saddle. 'I'm thinking maybe we ought to let these horses graze for an hour or so and me and you mosey in there on Shanks's mare.'

'I'll drink to that,' Joey muttered swinging down from his horse. Without a word he dragged the sawed-off shotgun from its short boot.

They staked the horses in a sparse patch of galleta grass and edged toward the mouth of the canyon in a crouch, moving only a few yards at a time and stopping often to look for any sign of alarm.

The falling rain muffled what little sound they made as they inched forward and, after half an hour of silent stalking, they dropped to their knees behind a thick stand of catclaw.

Auggie squinted at the steep walls of the canyon, thinking out loud, but softly enough that only Joey Benitez could hear.

'Let's see, now,' he mumbled, scanning the slope, 'if I was to put a rifleman up there, he would be right about . . . yep, there he is . . . brown-haired kid with a Winchester and I've seen him before.'

'I don't see him,' Joey whispered.

'Right beside that blue-gray boulder,' Augie said, pointing at the slope. 'Looks like he's half asleep.'

'OK, I see him now. I've seen him before, too, Auggie. He's the kid that runs errands for Keogh and he's dumber'n a sack full of rocks.'

'You think it's Keogh's men in here?' Augie asked incredulously.

'That'd be my guess. The kid definitely ain't any kind of lawman and he doesn't pack the gear to be a bounty hunter.'

Auggie nodded soberly. 'Makes sense to me. Jesus, what's the country coming to when a man like Charlie Keogh has to get a shavetail that young to do his fighting for him?'

His eyes were busy searching the dense ironwood thicket off to their left, and he was still thinking out loud.

'That would put another dry gulcher right in there somewhere, maybe down by that clump of prickly pear, but at least this one has enough sense to keep his head down.'

'You think they know we're here?'

'Hard to say,' Augie murmured. 'These would be gate men, to close us in the same as we do to the mustang herds when we run them into a box canyon, and that means the rest of them are farther in toward the tanks.'

Joey snorted softly. 'I'm starting to see what you mean about out-thinking them.'

'The next trick is getting past these two without raising a ruckus.'

'We'll manage.'

'You take the boy, Joey. I'm not so sure I could do it.'

'I can do it, no problem. After the way they cut the guys down back at the ranch, I say let's kill 'em all and let God sort 'em out.'

'You're a hard man, Joey Benitez. Anyone ever tell you that?'

'My wife,' the foreman said with a silly schoolboy grin. 'But that's the way she likes it.'

He watched Joey slip away into the mesquite, then turned his attention to the dry-gulcher he expected to find in the ironwood thicket across the wash.

His uncle Cyrus had taught him the lore of the woods, for he had been the hunter of the family. He'd taught him how to use the wind and light to his advantage, how to walk without snapping twigs or scuffing dry leaves, but nothing in life had prepared him for the Sonoran Desert, a fierce, raw land where one wrong step could cost a man his life, and frequently did.

Still, he was glad for the skill he did have and knew he would have to use every bit of it in the next few minutes. The falling rain would cut the visibility down and diminish any sound, but he would be laying his life on the line crossing the shallow wash.

He really didn't have a choice.

The odds were long that Keogh's men would spot him before he got close enough to do any damage, but he had to try.

Pushing himself up, he walked in a crouch ten yards closer to the wash, carrying the Peacemaker low in his hand, certain that any sudden movement would attract attention, and dropped to his knees again behind a clump of thornscrub.

There was no movement ahead of him, no sound, nothing that seemed out of place, but still he was on edge and felt the coppery taste of apprehension rise in his throat.

He held very still for a moment, studying the empty arroyo ahead of him, then moved forward again. Slowly.

After several minutes he spotted the bushwhacker — a faded red shirt showing in the shadows — relaxing on a slab of lava rock amid the creosote and cholla, gazing off into space as if he didn't have a care in the world.

And, in reality, he didn't.

A few more silent steps, a work-hardened hand across the nose and mouth, the other at the base of his skull, a strong, quick twist, and his neck snapped.

The man's legs twitched a few times as he withered, the saddle rifle slipped from his fingers, and he was gone.

Joey had been right. He was one of Keogh's men and Auggie had seen him around town a time or two.

He almost felt sorry for the old man lying at his feet.

From the looks of him, he'd had iron in his younger days, undoubtedly one of the men who'd tamed the West with blood, sweat, and blisters. That was long ago, however, and he hadn't aged gracefully. His clothes were threadbare, his boots down at the heels, and his hair an unkempt shock of grey.

And, after all the toil and trouble he must have seen, this was the payoff?

Somehow it didn't seem fair.

Still, the man would have killed him without hesitation. It would have been his way.

Auggie peered across the wash, grateful the brown-haired kid was no longer in sight, then picked up the movement of Joey sidling back down the slope between the boulders.

He waited in silence, scanning the

canyon ahead of them, until the foreman knelt down at his side.

'They're playing it pretty close to the chest, Auggie.'

'That's what I was thinking, too,' Auggie said quietly. 'What happened to the kid?'

'You don't want to know.'

'Yeah,' Auggie croaked, 'you're probably right. I want to bring the horses on in here, Joey, just in case we have to light out real sudden like.'

Joey nodded his understanding and pushed himself erect. 'I'll bring them up. Just sit tight for a few minutes.'

Auggie sat back on his heels, finger-combed his thick hair, and watched the slim vaquero slip away into the late afternoon sun.

Ahead of them, in the canyon, death awaited them with a patience known only to wild things.

And in the end it didn't matter.

In the West, any man who wouldn't stand up and fight for his honor was as good as dead, anyway.

10

Charlie Keogh broke a branch of brittle ironwood over his knee and fed it into the fire.

The shadow of the low hill west of them was steadily pushing into the narrow wash that held Papago Wells and he could already feel the chill of the night setting in.

It was typical of the desert, scorching hot during the day and colder than hell after dark.

And, at his age, he didn't handle the cold very well.

He wanted a bath. A bath and a change of clothes. Maybe some food with a little flavor to it and served on clean plates. Was that too much to ask? He was, after all, the richest man in the Ajo Valley, and it was no more than he deserved.

'Bacon and beans suit you tonight?'

Asa Hodges asked from the fire.

'Anything'd suit me tonight,' Keogh mumbled disgustedly. 'A shot of snakehead whiskey. A brown-eyed girl. A feather bed . . . '

'Yeah, well, we're fresh out of luxuries. How's about a cup of Arbuckle's best instead?'

'Do I have a choice?'

Hodges snorted quietly. 'Not much of one. We're not exactly on a Sunday afternoon picnic here.'

The Copper King lifted a hand to stop Hodges' rambling and let his mind wander instead to the day this trouble had started.

The set-up at the mine had been so perfect.

No one was going to miss Ram Garza, and Auggie had walked right into it. The teamsters had descended upon him in all their righteous anger after the shooting, just as he had known they would — after all, Garza was one of them, wasn't he? — and this stinking gringo had shot him down in cold blood?

He was reasonably sure no one had seen him walk away from the window: possibly Gil Torres from the rooftop, but there could not have been anyone else.

As far as he knew they hadn't even been aware he was there, and he'd sat his horse back in the mesquite thicket until they had Kellerman trussed up on the floor of an ore wagon and were on their way to Tucson.

Ahh, yes, that had been sweet!

The judge in Tucson had been well aware which side of his bread had butter on it and the sentence had been a foregone conclusion.

Murder? One of Charlie Keogh's men? Not while he was on the bench, by God.

Death by hanging.

How could it have been anything else?

The dark-haired Santee paced quietly into their makeshift camp and lowered himself to sit on a chunk of rock against the steep wall of the arroyo. 'It's

138

starting to rain.'

Keogh wagged his head dubiously and lifted his gaze to the gunman.

'Now that's something we hadn't quite figured out.'

Santee met his eyes with a poisonous look, and there was a strong taste of bitterness in his voice.

'One of these days, Keogh,' he rumbled, 'you're going to let your alligator mouth overload your canary ass and you'd better hope I'm not around when that day comes.'

★ ★ ★

Auggie checked the load in the dead man's Winchester, then leaned back against the rocks and let his eyes slide shut. It had been a long day already and he knew it wasn't nearly over.

There were armed and dangerous men still ahead of them in the canyon, each one there for the sole purpose of planting him, and there was no doubt in his mind that they'd killed before.

Charlie Keogh would not have taken them on if there was any question about that.

It just wasn't his way.

He let his mind wander for a long moment. Back to the serenity of the ranch, the house, the kitchen, the friends.

They'd had just on 200 head of bangtails from the Coconino Plateau corralled in a tight box canyon just north of the ranch when all the trouble started. The vaqueros had been working with them for the better part of two months; earing them down, slapping a saddle on their backs, and one or the other of the Mexican bronc peelers climbing aboard.

Most of the horses were green-broke — would take a saddle and bridle quietly, but needed more work — and they'd been getting ready to drive them across the old Butterfield stage road to Las Cruces, then north to Santa Fe.

True enough the trail went straight through the heart of the Chiricahua

Apache country, but it avoided the worst of the mountains.

Even then there was a well-known buyer waiting for them in the sprawling pueblo of Santa Fe, and, at six dollars a head, it represented a sight of money.

It would have been enough to pay the crew their wages, enough to keep the ranch going. And now it was gone.

He clenched his teeth hard together thinking about it.

He owed Charlie Keogh for that one, too.

'I staked the horses back there in the thicket with those other two,' Joey said softly when he stepped back into view. 'Plenty of forage for them, but no water.'

'You ready for all this?'

'I was born ready. You want me up on that other slope again?'

Auggie nodded soberly and let his gaze swing back up the narrow rock defile. 'I think it's our best bet. You keep your head down when you're up there, Joey. Lupe would never forgive me if anything happened to you.'

'Yeah, well, she'd never forgive me, either. Keep the faith, *patrón*.'

Auggie watched his foreman sprint across the wash, disappear into the jumble of boulders on that side; then he pushed himself erect.

It was time to open the ball.

He edged through the ironwood thicket and worked his way slowly up the slope of the ridge where he crouched just below the crest, out of sight yet high enough that he had a wide view of the arroyo.

The wisp of whitish smoke rising ahead of him came from a tiny fire down in the shelter of the hollow, and he could hear the baritone voices of several men.

They didn't sound worried, but they weren't happy, either.

'Shoulda been here by now,' one grumbled.

'They'll get here,' another answered. 'They got no choice but to come in.'

'Well, I don't like it.'

'No one asked you to, *hombre*. Pull your horns in a little.'

'I'll pull your horns in, you jackass!'

'Any time you're feeling froggy, mister, just jump right in. I'm ready for you any time.'

That exchange was followed by some mumbled curses, but Auggie couldn't make out the words.

Narrowing his eyes, he picked out a route through the mesquite and cholla that would allow a reasonably safe passage to a spot directly above the fire if a man decided to try it.

The wet pumice soil would deaden any sound and there was enough brush that he'd be somewhat sheltered from view.

If a man moved slowly from where he stood, he could follow that indistinct path through the brush and rocks and put himself in position to fire down into the arroyo.

He'd have to be damned canny about it, but it could be done.

He worried his lower lip with his

teeth, rain peppering his face, and pondered making such a move.

Taking the battle to them would definitely wake them up to the fact that blood could be shed on both sides of the line they had drawn, that they had tangled with a man who would stand up and fight when push came to shove.

And, in reality, there wasn't any other way of going about it. For damned sure he didn't want to end up like the four bounty hunters who'd come on to them at Tule Tank.

He spotted Joey edging forward on the far side of the canyon, holding the scattergun high in front of his chest, and he made his decision.

It was root hog or die.

For a moment he just sat there among the oddly jointed clumps of prickly pear, letting his eyes become even more accustomed to the scant light, feeling the rain soak his shirt, then he rose to a crouch and started forward.

The arroyo was off to his right, perhaps ten yards away, and he inched forward a few paces at a time, keeping low, toward a scraggily stand of mesquite.

He spied the lookout posted in the high rocks behind the tanks easily enough, a square-shouldered man with ragged blond hair, but he was studying the desert floor some distance off, ignoring the approaches to the canyon, apparently not even aware that the danger was much closer.

And, strangely, the lookout's complacency seemed to fuel Auggie's own bravado.

He simply rose and walked to the edge of the ravine directly above the guttering fire.

They were down there all right, three of them, drinking coffee from tin cups and eyeing each other with as much disdain as it's possible to have short of bloodshed.

He stood stock still, waiting for something — anything — to happen, having no idea what it would be.

After a long moment one of them, a

man with hooded eyes and a bloodless face, lifted his gaze to the rim and spotted him.

'What the . . . '

He went for his gun and Auggie shot him.

The man was thrown backwards a yard or so, his six-shooter falling away, and landed flat on his back in the wet gravel of the arroyo, clawing at the gravel with both hands; then he lay still.

He watched the wine-red stain of blood spread across the chest of the man's shirt for a split second, then spun on his heel and dove for cover behind a chunk of bluish lava rock.

Those men down there had learned something just now.

The hard way.

A hail of gunfire racketed over his head but he was out of sight of the men on the floor of the wash. The only one who really had a shot at him was the blond gunman in the rocks across the notch.

He heard the dull roar of Joey's

10-gauge from the other side of the arroyo then and the hail of gunfire shifted to that side of the canyon.

Glancing quickly over his shoulder, he saw Joey throw up his arms and sink among the rocks, apparently hit; he turned his attention back to the lookout.

The blond gunman lifted his head for a moment, apparently trying to spot Joey again, and that was all Auggie needed.

His shot took the man just below the eye and came out of the back of his head.

He slumped into the cholla, his Winchester clattering against the ancient lava rocks, and a sudden, shocking hush settled over Papago Wells.

11

Damn him!

Keogh clamped his teeth hard together and glowered at the empty rim of the arroyo.

This mustang man, this August Kellerman, was beginning to chap his hide. Really hard.

He'd come from nowhere, in the middle of a rainstorm, faced down one of his hired gun hands, a known and deliberate killer, and had dropped him where he stood.

There'd been no fear in him, no quit, and he'd done it as if it were nothing more than a daily chore, like chopping kindling or carrying water from the well.

Keogh glanced around at Asa Hodges. At least three of them were already gone . . . old Buck Renner and the kid, for it would have been impossible for

Kellerman to get this deep into the canyon without cutting them down first . . . and, strangely, he didn't count them as any big loss.

Now it was Santee.

He was no closer to killing Kellerman than he had been at this same time yesterday.

Damn it! Could none of these people do anything right?

It was starting to look like, if he wanted this thing done, he would have to do it himself.

And that chapped his hide, too.

'Call Briscoe down,' he growled at Hodges. 'I think it's time we ride out of here.'

Hodges huffed at his order.

'I swear, Keogh, you are one dumb bastard. Harry Briscoe is dead. So are the rest of them and I've got buckshot in my leg.'

'You're hit?' Keogh blurted.

'There were two of them. Or didn't you happen to notice? Kellerman on one side and a Mex with a shotgun on the other. I took the Mex down with a lucky shot, but not before he got some lead into me.'

The Copper King took a deep breath and exhaled it heavily.

'So what do we do now?'

'We hightail it out of here, you lame brain. Or would you rather just sit here and wait your turn to die?'

Keogh glared at the hostler in the shelter of the rocks. He was not in the habit of being insulted. By anyone.

'I don't like the way you speak to me, Hodges. When we get back to Ajo, you can draw your pay and move on.'

'Tell you what, bossman, you give me my time and I'll move on right now. We'll see if you can make it back to town on your own.'

'Don't be absurd,' Keogh groused. 'You know I can't.'

'Then help me on to a horse, fall in behind me, and keep your pie hole shut. Much more of your stupidity tonight and I'll shoot you myself.'

★ ★ ★

A saddle creaked and Auggie heard the unmistakable clatter of hoofs going through the narrow notch in the rocks. Still, he stayed put until the sound had disappeared into the night.

A parting shot would only have wasted a bullet.

When he was sure they were gone he picked his way back down the slope, leaned the Winchester against a rock by the fire, and scrambled up the other side to where he'd seen Joey fall.

He had no idea what he could say to Lupe about Joey's death. They were too close to be evasive about it and it just made no sense at all that he was gone.

Joey's introduction to bronc-busting was almost legend among the family, and Auggie had heard the story many, many times over the years they'd been together.

He'd guided General Jo Shelby, the Confederate General who refused to surrender at the end of the Civil War, to

Mexico City to meet with Maximilian when he crossed into Mexico with 1,000 men at Eagle Pass, Texas, and was well thought of by the rugged men of the undefeated Missouri Iron Brigade.

Of course, the Austrian pretender hadn't been interested in dealing with a force the size of Shelby's, and he had declined his services.

With the end of the brigade clearly in sight, Jo Shelby returned to the Rio Grande, where he'd sunk the brigade's battle flag in the river, divided the treasury among the men — fifty dollars for each man regardless of rank — allowed them to take their horse, arms, all of their equipment, and paroled them from the service some five months after General Lee surrendered at Appomattox Court House.

The story was that one of Shelby's men, a burly sergeant named Alonzo Dedham, had a coal black stallion that would allow absolutely no one to ride him except the sergeant, and, apparently, that was Sergeant Dedham's big brag.

Almost as a joke, he'd bet Joey a ten-dollar gold piece that he couldn't ride him, and Joey, unaware of the horse's reputation, had accepted.

They said fully half the brigade, as well as most of Joey's family, had gathered to watch the spectacle when he climbed aboard the horse, and what a show they got.

The black sunfished into the shape of a crescent, frog-walked, squealed and kicked its way around the corral, and, somehow, incredibly, Joey was staying on his back.

The bucks grew higher as the contest continued, a cloud of choking dust rose around them, neither horse nor rider willing to give an inch, as if their very life depended on defeating the other.

After half an hour the bucking slowed and became weaker, the black trotted around the corral, tossing his head, flinging kicks at the men on the fence, and finally stood with his head hanging, nostrils distended, gasping for air. Joey Benitez had ridden him to an unbelievable standstill.

Sergeant Dedham gave him the ten-dollar gold piece, just as he'd said, along with a handshake and an honest pat on the back, and, when he led a crew of men off toward the Llano Estacado to go mustanging, he asked Joey to ride with them.

It meant the start of a career for Joey Benitez, a way to support his family, a way to hold his head up, and he had jumped at the chance.

Auggie found his body in the darkness, sprawled across a slab of broken rock. He clamped his eyes shut at the sight, and choked back the groan of despair forming deep in his throat.

'God damn it, Joey. Why couldn't it have been me?'

'Easy, Auggie,' came a coarse voice below him. 'I'm not dead but I think I'm in trouble.'

Auggie's eyes snapped open and his breath caught in his throat at the words.

'Joey?'

'Can you get me down out of here?'

'You're damned right I can. Hang on.'

As carefully as he could, he slung the gutsy bronc buster over his shoulder, picked his scattergun up out of the shadows, and eased his way back down through the rocks and jumping cholla to the makeshift campsite.

He hunkered down near the guttering fire Keogh's man had put together and lowered his foreman to a stretch of soft sand.

The night around them was black as a hangman's hood except for the occasional, distant flash of heat lightning.

'Took you through the shoulder, Joey,' he rasped, studying the wound by the light of an ironwood torch. 'I'll have to cauterize this to stop the bleeding.'

'I was afraid you were going to say that.'

They both knew that cauterizing a bullet wound such as this was a painful proceeding, and here, with nothing to minimize the pain, it would come down to a matter of grit.

Either you had it or you didn't.

'I don't think we have much choice, Joey. I'm pretty sure you've got some broken bones in there, but the bullet came all the way through. I don't think there are any organs in there to worry about, either. Our main concern right now is to stop the flow of blood.'

'You ever do this before, *jefe*?' Joey asked, looking him squarely in the eyes.

Auggie shook his head at the question and lowered the torch. 'No, but I saw it done a couple of times during the war. You got a Bowie knife on you?'

'Got an Arkansas toothpick in my boot. That do?'

'Anything will do. I just need something to heat up. And don't worry, my friend, it doesn't have to be white hot. Just hot enough to close the wound.'

Joey leaned back against the rock and

peered away into the darkness. 'Better get me a stick to bite on, Auggie, and if you ever tell anyone I screamed when we did this, I'm going to kick your ass.'

Auggie snorted quietly at his foreman's threat. 'I've got way too much respect for you to do something stupid like that, my friend, and to be totally honest with you, I'm not so sure I could do this at all.'

'I trust you,' Joey croaked. He glanced down toward the knife in his boot and attempted a smile. It did not look genuine. 'Let's get it done.'

Auggie nodded his agreement, dragged the straight-bladed throwing knife out of its hidden boot scabbard, and tested the edge with his thumb almost as a reflex action.

He picked up an ironwood branch from the pile of firewood, cut a short piece, handed it to the slender vaquero, and shoved the blade of the knife into the coals.

'I wish I had some whiskey I could

give you, Joey, but I don't. I'll be as quick as I can.'

'I know,' Joey said evenly. 'I'm ready when you are.'

Auggie waited a brief moment, pulled the knife from the fire, and shrugged his shoulders. There was no way to judge whether it would be hot enough, it would be just a wild guess on his part, but that was all he could do.

'This is going to hurt.'

Joey bobbed his head again, clamped down on the stick between his teeth, and Auggie touched the flat of the glowing blade to the wound.

The sickening-sweet smell of burning blood and flesh assailed their nostrils at the touch. He heard Joey's sharp intake of breath and the groan from deep in his chest.

'Nnnnggghhhhh!'

His eyes rolled up suddenly, his head lolled back against the rock, and he was out cold.

Auggie held the ironwood torch up quickly to examine his work and breathed easier, seeing that the ooze of blood from the entry wound had stopped. As gently as he could, he pulled Joey's body forward against his own chest and touched the knife blade to the exit wound in back.

The acrid smell hit him again as he lowered the blade, and he exhaled heavily.

It was done.

A surge of relief washed over him, and he held Joey's body close against himself, rocking him slowly like a devoted father would comfort a sick child.

'Aw, you poor bastard,' he murmured. 'I'm glad you passed out.'

He lowered the foreman carefully to the sand and covered him against the coming chill of the desert night with a blanket that Keogh's man had left behind.

Then, more to settle his own nerves than anything else, he poured a cup of hot, black coffee from the dented pot on the rocks, took a deep swig of it, and stared away into the dark.

He scooted back against the rocks and laid the saddle rifle within easy reach across his legs.

Some things a man learned very quickly in the West; you kept your gun loaded all the time, you drank when there was water, and you rested when you could.

Beyond that, you got by the best you knew how.

The rustle of dry leaves in the ironwood thicket as some small animal scampered through searching for food, and the heavy wing beats of a hunting owl told him there was no further threat to them in the narrow canyon.

Still, with this many people out gunning for him, he knew there'd be no sleep tonight.

And that was just the way of it.

He lowered his face into the palms of his hands, ignoring the rivulet of rainwater that trickled off the brim of his hat, and tried to concentrate on the problem he had with the Copper King.

Keogh had already shown the way he did things and the odds were keen that he'd do it the exact same way again. He would undoubtedly have bushwhackers at every vantage point on the way into Ajo, while he himself would be barricaded behind closed doors somewhere with half a dozen more hired guns protecting him in there.

Yet Auggie felt sure there was a chink in his plan. There had to be. Some small weakness that even Charlie Keogh had not considered.

It was like Joey always told him: there was never a rider that couldn't be throwed, and never a horse that couldn't be rode.

And suddenly — like a revelation from God — it came to him.

The way to beat the Copper King was simply to play his own game!

If he could get to Ajo before Keogh had time to pick out the vantage points, before he had time to select the fields of fire and set up his ambushers; if he could be in position to attack before

Keogh even knew he was there . . .

Yes!

The whole trick was in the timing.

He squeezed his eyes shut, trying to remember the faint trail across the desert and up through Growler Pass.

It would be tricky with only flashes of lightning to see by and it was spitting rain to boot, but, all things considered, he figured they had a better than fifty-fifty chance of making it back to town in one piece.

It was the first ray of hope he'd had since he'd gotten away from Jack Raley.

He reached around and tapped Joey's leg through the blanket.

'Joey. You awake?'

'Yeah,' the vaquero croaked.

'How are you feeling?'

'Not so good. What's on your mind?'

Auggie hesitated a moment before answering, hoping beyond hope that his foreman was alert enough to comprehend.

'I'm thinking if we can to get into town before Keogh has a chance to set up we might be able to even the odds in this thing a little.'

Joey pushed himself up to a sitting position, wincing at the pain in his shoulder, and met Auggie's eyes with sudden interest. 'He damned sure wouldn't be expecting that, would he?'

'You think you can ride?'

'I can ride,' Joey said grimly. 'I can shoot, too.'

'No, the fight's over for you, my friend. I want to get you to Doc Curran's place and that's where you're going to stay. This is between me and Charlie Keogh.'

'I owe that son of a bitch, Auggie.'

'You can piss on his grave.'

'Now who's being hard?'

Auggie lifted his hands in resignation but didn't avert his eyes. 'Sorry. That's the way it is. I want to bind you up with some strips of blanket so you can't move around too much, then we'll see about getting you on a horse.'

'Any coffee left in there?' Joey asked,

nodding toward the blackened coffee pot.

'Almost a full pot. Black as sin and it's strong enough to float a horseshoe. You want a cup?'

'I could use it. Catching rainwater in my hands on the ridge up there didn't quite get the job done.'

Auggie sloshed half a cup of coffee around in one of the tin cups that had been left to rinse it out, filled it to the brim, and handed it to his foreman without speaking.

He cut a couple of two-inch strips off the soggy blanket Keogh's man had left and wrapped them around Joey's torso tight enough to bind the limp arm to his side, but not tight enough to cut off the circulation.

'You get the blood stopped?'

Auggie nodded soberly. 'I got it, but it's a long ride to Ajo.'

'Then we'd better make tracks out of here before it opens up again.'

'I'll bring the horses up,' Auggie said. 'They can drink their fill while you get your head screwed on straight and we'll head out. This ain't going to be a walk around the plaza.'

'At least we're still walking.'

'Yeah,' Auggie muttered, 'but for how long?'

12

The Copper King pulled the slicker tighter about himself and tugged his hat brim down to keep the raindrops from hitting his face. Lightning crackled in the distance and thunder rumbled across the desert in a sullen, muted response.

He caught only occasional glimpses of Hodges even though the man was not that far ahead of him, but he made no effort at all to catch up, just gave the dun his head and let him do what he did best.

He had underestimated Kellerman, he realized that now, and he was having a little difficulty grasping the fact that this simple damned bronc buster had taken his entire crew down as if they were targets in a shooting gallery.

The man had surprised him, no doubt about it.

And that took some doing.

He'd seen men who could handle a gun in every seamy rat hole from Bald Knob on the Ohio River to San Francisco's infamous Barbary Coast, and this August Kellerman would have to take a back seat to none of them.

He realized, too, that he needed a new strategy.

Kellerman was not going down without a fight, not going to roll over and play 'dead dog' for him, and that meant trouble.

He felt reasonably sure that setting up a simple barricade for him in Ajo was just not going to be enough. From what he'd seen at Papago Wells, dry-gulchers didn't even slow the man down.

No, he had to think this one out.

He clamped his teeth hard together and banged his mouth with the side of a doubled fist, forcing himself to look past the obvious on this problem.

Realistically, the only way Kellerman could turn this thing around was to find out if the lookout, Gil Torres, had seen anything on the day that Ramiro Garza died.

If he had and Kellerman could make him spill it, it marked the end of the run for Charlie Keogh.

If he hadn't it marked the end of the run for Auggie Kellerman. The Copper King had to find the answer to the question first.

Still, he mused, there was another way.

If Gil Torres was no longer available — dead, for example — it would be damned difficult for Kellerman to find out anything at all.

Impossible, as a matter of fact.

And the Copper King definitely liked the sound of that.

It could be any number of things — an accident at the mine, a horse throwing him, a gunman who just didn't like greasers — and who'd be the wiser?

Yes, there were some definite possibilities in this line of thinking.

It would take a little planning, true enough, but it was a way out.

He was anxious to get to town now, anxious to see what would come of this, cursing, under his breath the night and the rain.

He spurred the dun into a little faster gait, reining in just short of Asa Hodges, and glared at the man's broad back.

Could he possibly go any slower?

★　★　★

Auggie dug a black rain slicker from Joey's saddlebag, draped it over his shoulders, and buttoned the top few buttons.

'You sure you can stay in the saddle?'

Joey snorted indignantly at his question and pulled himself up on to the paint with his one good arm.

'You'll never see the day I have to grab the apple, *jefe*,' he rasped, but he said it through clenched teeth and Auggie knew he was in pain.

169

'Yeah, well, I want you close by just in case. I'm going to take us out the way we came in. I've never been through that notch in the rocks and I don't trust it in the dark.'

'Sounds like a plan to me. Let's ride.'

Without another word Auggie picked up Joey's reins, tugged the sorrel's head around toward the foot of the canyon, and nudged her into a slow walk.

His mind went back to the day he'd come upon Joey and that bunch of salty mustangers on the Llano Estacado. The day that had turned his life around.

He remembered the land out there had been as flat and monotonous as a tabletop. Not a tree nor a bush in sight, just the dusty brown grass as far as a man could ride, as if you could stand up in your stirrups and see tomorrow.

He remembered, too, the bandy-legged little *vaquero* with the appraising look in his eyes approaching him.

'You looking for work?'

'Sure am,' he'd said. 'Work and maybe a hot meal.'

'You're in luck then, mister. We got both. You ever stomp broncos?'

'No, but I'm a quick learner.'

'You damn well better be,' the wiry Mexican had muttered. 'Bronc-peelers are usually washed up by the age of thirty, all busted up inside from riding the snuffy ones, so you got to make hay while the sun shines.'

'What do you pay?'

'Thirty a month and found. And don't worry, you'll earn every damned dollar of it.'

The very first thing Joey had taught him was how to fall. How to kick free of the stirrups, to go limp and hit the ground rolling, for it was not the getting thrown part that worried a bronc buster, but the thought of his foot becoming hung in the stirrup and finding himself under a man-killer's hoofs.

That had been only the start of his education. He'd found, as had every other mustang man throughout history, that he had to have almost a sixth sense

171

about the horses he topped, knowing which way the horse was going to jump next, knowing he was going to chew gravel a step or two before he actually went down.

He'd been grassed several times those first few days, much to the amusement of the experienced peelers, but he'd gotten back up every single time, checking his body for broken bones under the pretense of dusting himself off, and climbed back aboard the animal that had dumped him.

He was skinned and bruised and sore in muscles he didn't even know he had, but there was no quit in him.

Never had been.

His determination alone, it seemed, had put him in the good graces of the other riders and, by the end of the round-up, Joey had taken him on full time.

It was only because he was a gringo, commanding slightly more respect in the Territory than the Mexicans would, that he was pushed into the position of being *jefe*, or boss, of their little outfit.

It wasn't something he'd wanted, but, now that he had it, he did his level best to make the business pay off for them.

Joey had been named foreman but the reality of it was they were virtually partners.

Most people pictured wild-horse herds as being led around by the stallion when, in fact, almost the exact opposite was true. Each herd had a dominant mare who led the family group in their grazing, to the water hole, and to sheltered places out of the wind when storms howled across the desert.

The stallion was normally in the rear, protecting the group from attack by another stallion or a predator. He usually stood guard, keenly alert and positioned slightly away from the group. If any perceived threat approached them, the stallion would place himself in front of his band and challenge the intruder.

Deer and pronghorn antelope often grazed near a band of mustangs because they knew the stallion would alert them to any danger.

And their life was not easy.

The fact of the matter was that there was hardly another critter on God's green earth that lived a more miserable life than a wild horse. Their manes and tails were usually a tangled mess of snarls, knots, burrs and stickers, and they lived scared, always in danger, had a lot of pain, and died young.

Truth be known, their lives got a hell of a lot better once they did come under the care of humans, whether they were broken to the saddle or simply pulling a wagon somewhere. At least they were fed and watered on a regular basis and predators were kept at a distance.

Idealists to the contrary, that's the way it was.

Auggie swung the sorrel around the huge boulders at the foot of the wash, keeping the Agua Dulce range on his right by the sporadic flashes of lightning sparking across the desert.

The trail was only dimly visible in the night, a worn space between the clumps of mesquite, but he filed into it and nudged the mare into a little faster gait.

'You OK, Joey?' he asked over his shoulder.

'So far,' his foreman moaned, 'but I've damned sure been better.'

'Let me know if you need a breather. We can always stop if it comes to that.'

'You get my shotgun?'

'It's in the boot,' he said, 'but I didn't have a chance to reload it.'

'Might have to before we get to town.'

'Just ride easy. We'll deal with problems as they come our way.'

'I've never been shot before, Auggie,' the foreman mumbled. 'You think I'm going to be OK?'

Auggie shrugged in the dark, knowing Joey couldn't see it, and attempted to keep the worry out of his voice.

'I'm no hand at doctoring, Joey, but I

saw a lot of gunshot wounds during the war. A lot of them were worse than yours, torn up by minie balls, you know? And most of them survived.'

'Most of them? What the hell is that supposed to mean?'

'It means you fret too much.'

Joey snorted loudly. 'You're a lot of help.'

'I don't know what you want me to say,' Auggie groused. 'Chances are there'll be some movements you can't make as good as you did before, but I don't think it'll slow you down none. For right now I just want you to keep your chin up and hang on. We'll be at the doctor's place in a couple of hours and he can tell you better than I can.'

'Remind me to kick your ass when I get my strength back.'

'Nothing to worry about then,' he said with a low chuckle. 'That's one movement you never were any good at.'

A low wind trembled the palo verde leaves around them and Auggie picked

Growler Pass out in the occasional flash of lightning shimmering across the desert. He tugged the sorrel around more in that direction, patted her neck to calm her, and pushed on to the northeast.

He knew when they passed the ranch site in the darkness. The acrid odor of charred timber, a smell that lingered for weeks after a burn and was always brought back to life again by dampness or rainfall, hung heavily on the air and there was no mistaking it.

He clenched his teeth hard together, remembering again the hours of work they'd put into building the place, remembering the devil-take-tomorrow vaqueros who had died there.

The very thought of it grated on him and he steeled himself for what lay ahead.

This would all come to a head tomorrow and Charlie Keogh had a lot to answer for.

More than likely it would come down to a bloody shoot-out with the Copper

King's men, and there was no guarantee that Auggie would walk away from it.

Still, he thought, he had it to do.

13

The rain let up sometime after midnight and the few pale stars peeking through the clouds were hanging low in the sky by the time they rode over the ridge into Ajo.

There was only one light showing in town, fanning out on to the street from the streaked window of the saloon, but Auggie doubted anyone was in there.

Not at this hour.

Still, he avoided the place, riding instead to the back of Doc Curran's residence, where he tied the horses to the porch rail.

He pulled Joey's weight sideways into his arms, plodded up the dark steps, and tapped on the doctor's door with his boot.

A few minutes passed before a fan of yellowish lantern light leaked out beneath the door and graying-at-the-temples Doctor

Sam Curran swung the door open.

'Auggie?' he asked incredulously. 'I wasn't so sure I'd see you again. Seems like half the Territory is hunting you.'

'I've got a wounded man here, Sam,' Auggie mumbled. 'Can you take a look at him?'

'Sure,' the doctor said, holding the door open. 'That's what I'm here for. Set him on that table right there and get his slicker and those strips of blanket off. This is your foreman, isn't it?'

'Yeah,' Auggie replied, peeling the raincoat from Joey's back. 'Joey Benitez.'

'Gunshot?'

Auggie nodded. 'Happened earlier last evening and we rode all night to get here. I cauterized it the best I could, but I'm afraid it's a half-assed job.'

The doctor looked up from examining the wound by the light of the lantern and met his gaze evenly. 'Actually it's a pretty good job, Auggie. The exit wound has opened up again but the entry is still OK. He's got some bone fragments in there I'll have to get out, but I think he'll survive.'

He peered closely into Joey's heavy eyes and asked the obvious question. 'How are you feeling, Joey?'

'Not so good. You got anything for pain?'

'I'll mix something for you.'

'Might be a good idea to close your curtains, too, Doc,' Auggie said, glancing around the small room. 'I'm not real anxious for people to know I'm here.'

'I wouldn't doubt that. The news of your escape came in day before yesterday and they said there was a reward out for you.'

'You're not wanting to collect it, are you?'

'Aw, you should know me better than that. You're the one man around here I had any respect for.' The doctor paced across to the windows, pulled the curtains tight together, then busied himself at a small counter in the corner.

He turned after several minutes and

held a glass of amber liquid up to the light.

'I'm going to give your foreman some laudanum to kill the pain — opium mixed with whiskey — but the stuff is really addictive so I don't want him to have very much of it. A couple of spoonfuls will be about it and he's not going to be busting any broncos for a while.'

'I can live with that. He's going to be all right, though?'

'Oh, yeah. He's young and strong. Got a lot more years in him.'

He studied Auggie's haggard face and narrowed his eyes. 'You look like you could use some rest.'

'I am tired.'

'Well, I don't have a spare bed, but you're welcome to the sofa over there.' Curran jerked his head toward Joey again and continued: 'This is going to take some time. If you want, I can wake you when I'm finished.'

'That'd be good. You know why I'm here, don't you, Sam?'

Curran shrugged but didn't look away. 'I'm not absolutely certain, but I'm guessing it has something to do with Charlie Keogh.'

'You got that part right.'

'He's not your only problem, Auggie. That deputy marshal you got away from is here in town, too. Word is he's staying at the Maricopa House hotel and is none too happy with you.'

'That I'd believe,' Auggie mumbled. 'I fetched him a clout on the side of the head with a piece of shackle chain. Probably still has a headache from it.'

'You ready for this, Joey?' Curran mumbled, handing Joey the glass.

Auggie watched his foreman toss the medicine down with his one good hand, exhale heavily, and let his eyes slide shut.

'Got a little good news for you, too,' the doctor said quietly. 'Joey's wife and another woman were with the deputy when he got down off the stage from Yuma yesterday. I thought I recognized her from seeing her around town, and, now that Joey's here, I'm sure it's her.'

'Lupe's here?' Joey blurted.

'I'm pretty sure it's her. Word is they took a room at the hotel, same as the deputy.'

'Any chance of getting them over here without being seen, Sam?' Auggie asked. 'I'm betting it would make Joey feel better and I imagine Lupe's pretty worried right now.'

Curran nodded his understanding. 'I'll send my housekeeper after them. In the meantime, you need to get some sleep and I need to get started picking the bones out of this wound. There's coffee on the stove, if you want some.'

'I'll settle for the sleep, Doc. I've got a real strong feeling I'm going to need my wits about me come morning.'

Even as he said it, he knew sleep wouldn't come. He was too keyed up for that and there was a good chance he'd get to see pretty Becky Camacho again before morning.

Still, he lowered himself to the doctor's velveteen sofa, pushed the bullet-torn hat down over his face, and closed his eyes.

It had been a long ride from Tinajas Altas. Long and tiring and full of bloodshed.

And it wasn't nearly over.

Somewhere in town, he knew, Charlie Keogh, the Copper King of Arizona, was just beginning to stir, just beginning to form his strategy, and things didn't bode well for Auggie Kellerman.

He was in this alone now and had no idea how to go about clearing his name.

He was reasonably sure someone at the mine must have seen Keogh the morning Ram Garza died; a lookout, perhaps — and he knew Keogh had three or four of them — maybe a teamster standing around waiting for his wagon to be loaded, a miner or one of the Mexican roustabouts shoveling ore into the carts.

It was impossible to believe that not one single person on the entire site wouldn't have seen him ride in or out that day, but how to ferret them out?

There wasn't a lot of time.

He started ticking off the number of men who had already died as a result of Keogh's greed, almost subconsciously lifting a finger for each one he counted.

And every one of those deaths could be laid squarely at Charlie Keogh's door.

The truly disheartening part was that there were going to be even more when he finally went after the Copper King.

There was no way to avoid it.

And the odds were pretty short that Auggie would be among them.

*   *   *

The Copper King was not in a good mood. He hadn't had nearly enough sleep and he was a man who appreciated his comfort.

His first act on coming downstairs was to give a month's pay for Asa Hodges to the cook with instructions to pay him off when he came in for breakfast and send him on his way.

He wanted no more of the man's insolence, and he was ending it as curtly as he knew how.

Picking a soda biscuit from the platter on the counter, he smeared a pat of butter on it with one of the sterling kitchen knives, and paced out with a self-satisfied smirk.

Sass him back, would he?

Not in this lifetime.

Pulling his bowler hat a little lower over his eyes, he marched down the narrow street to the tiny board-and-bat mine office.

His men were all at work when he stepped through the door, or at least they seemed to be, and he wasted no time on exchanging pleasantries with them.

Instead, he pushed open the door to his small office and paced in.

'Send Gil Torres in here,' Keogh barked at the balding clerk.

He took a seat in the cracked cordovan leather chair, propped his feet up on the desk, laced his fingers across his belly, and waited.

It was time to find out where he stood in all this once and for all.

It was only a matter of minutes before the lookout tapped on his door. He looked up with jaundiced eyes.

'Come!'

'You wanted to see me, Mister Keogh?' The slender *peón* asked, holding his battered straw hat in his hands.

'Yes. You were on the rooftop the day Garza was killed weren't you?'

'*Sí*, and I wasn't asleep, either.'

'I wondered about that,' the Copper King rumbled. 'So then, did you see anything out of the ordinary?'

Torres grinned at him and relaxed visibly. 'Are you asking if I saw you, *patrón*?'

'From your answer, I'm guessing that you did.'

'*Sí*, I saw you walk away from the window after the shot and I saw you waiting in the brush until the teamsters had Kellerman in the ore cart and drove out.'

'Why didn't you say anything?'

Torres cocked his head, still grinning. 'I had an idea my silence might be worth something.'

Keogh sat up straight then, tenting his fingers on the desktop. 'You mean you planned on blackmailing me?'

'Aww, *patrón*,' the lookout crooned, 'blackmail is such a hard word. I prefer to think of it as a *cambio*, an exchange, you know? My silence in exchange for some of your money?'

Keogh pushed himself erect and paced around the desk, turning a short, gleaming dagger over and over in his hand.

'You wife is with child, isn't she, Gil?'

'*Sí*. Eight months.'

The lookout backed away from him even as he spoke, his eyes wide with apprehension and fixed on the dagger.

And, without batting an eye, Keogh drove the knife to the hilt into the lookout's lean belly.

Torres grimaced quickly, doubled

over in pain, and groaned deep in his throat.

'Do you have any idea, Mister Torres,' Keogh mumbled, 'how easy it would be for me to do this to your wife? Do you have any idea what that would do to the baby?'

'You wouldn't dare.'

'Wouldn't I?' he asked. 'Are you willing to bet your baby's life on it?'

He hesitated a long moment, letting the gruesome picture of a dagger sinking into his wife's protruding belly take root in the lookout's mind.

'Now, then,' he said eventually, 'about our little *cambio*. How about your silence in exchange for some of my mercy?'

Torres nodded, perspiration suddenly beading on his cheeks and forehead. '*Sí*, I will be quiet. But you leave my Consuela alone.'

'You really should have that looked at,' Keogh muttered, nodding toward the knife wound in the lookout's stomach.

He turned, that same self-satisfied smirk working its way across his thin lips again, and sauntered out.

Torres would be too afraid to open his mouth now, he was absolutely sure of that, and it was time for other things.

Time for a shot of bourbon. Time for some planning. Time to get August Kellerman out of his life forever.

Finally this mess would be over and he could start thinking seriously about turning the day-to-day operation of the mine over to a manager and getting the hell out of this miserable country.

It couldn't come too soon.

Behind him Gil Torres staggered to the office door and swung it open, blood drooling down the front of his worn grey trousers, and called quietly to one of his friends.

'*Oye, compadre,*' he croaked. 'Tell that marshal staying at the hotel I've got something to tell him.'

'*Ay caramba, hombre!*' his friend hissed. 'What happened?'

'Just get the marshal,' Gil said

191

clutching the stab wound in his belly a little tighter. 'Maybe I'm nothing more than a lookout for this *pendejo*, but he is not going to threaten my family.'

14

They heard the women talking for a moment on the doctor's shadowed back porch, then the door swung open and the women pushed their way into the treatment room: Joey's stocky little wife, pretty Becky Camacho, and another heavyset Mexican woman whom Auggie could only assume was Sam Curran's housekeeper.

'Oh, my God, Joey,' Lupe gasped as she scurried in, 'are you OK? Is he OK, doctor?'

'He's been shot, Mrs . . . ?'

'Benitez,' Auggie offered.

' . . . Mrs Benitez. He's lost a lot of blood but he'll be all right.'

She rushed to the side of the table, lay her hand carefully on her husband's bare back, and leaned down close to his ear.

'Did you hear that, *mi amor*? The

doctor says you'll be all right.'

'I hear you, woman,' the foreman groaned. 'I'm glad you're here.'

She lifted her gaze to Auggie and attempted a smile. 'And you, *hijo*,' she asked quietly, 'are you OK?'

'I'm all right. We ran into a couple of gunfights on the way here, but we dished out more than we took.'

Becky pushed her way past them to Auggie's side, hugged him close against her, then stepped away in deference to the strict old Mexican customs which the family still observed.

'You sure you're OK, Auggie?' she asked softly. 'No bullet holes in you this morning?'

'Not so far.'

'And what is that supposed to mean?'

'It means I've still got a fight on my hands.'

'You don't have to do this, you know?' she murmured. 'You could just walk away from this madness. We can start over in California, like you told Joey.'

He shook his head somberly at her proposal. 'No, I have to see this through. A lot of men are already dead because of what Charlie Keogh did, and it's time he pays the freight.'

'But it doesn't have to be you who collects it.'

She lowered her eyes to the braided rugs covering the treatment room floor, as if searching for the right words, then lifted her chin defiantly and met his gaze again.

'I love you, Auggie. I have since the first time I saw you and the whole family knows it. I want to have children, lots of children, and I want you to be their father.'

'I love you, too, Becky, but — '

'If you walk into this fight with Keogh, there's a good chance you won't be coming back and I'd rather have you alive. I'll be a good wife to you, I promise. We'll have a good life together.'

The words rushed past him in an urgent, Mexican-flavored whisper, and he smiled grimly at her concern.

He understood pride, could appreciate what it had cost her to utter those words, especially in front of the others, still he couldn't bring himself to back down.

'And what kind of life would that be? Every time you looked at me from now on, you'd remember that I am the man who wouldn't stand up and fight for his honor.'

He hesitated momentarily then added, 'This is something I have to do. I don't go looking for trouble and you know it, but I don't walk away from it, either.'

'Men!' she hissed. 'Why are men so hard-headed about such things?'

'It's because we have to look at ourselves in a shaving mirror every once in a while.'

Behind her Lupe leaned down over the doctor's marred table, seemingly content that her husband was still in one piece.

'Joey,' she whispered, 'when's the last time the two of you ate?'

'Yesterday morning,' he replied weakly. 'Your chorizo and beans.'

She turned on her heel, started talking to the doctor's housekeeper in rapid Spanish, and nodded a quick invitation to her kid sister. 'Help us in the kitchen, Becky. We're going to cook breakfast for everyone.'

The graying doctor helped Joey up to a sitting position after the women had left the room, wiped the dried blood off his back with a damp towel and put a dressing on the wound.

'There's not much more I can do for you right now, Joey,' he said evenly. 'You'll have to take it easy for a while, give this thing a chance to heal up and get your strength back.'

'Be glad to oblige,' Joey croaked.

'I don't know when I can pay you for all this, Sam,' Auggie ventured across the table.

'Don't worry about it,' Curran replied. 'Buy me a drink sometime.'

'I can do that. Just tell me when you're ready.'

He glanced across toward the kitchen door, suddenly conscious of how ragged he must look, and remembered what he'd just said to Becky about looking in a mirror.

'Would you happen to have a spare razor I could get next to, Sam?'

'That little lady in there allergic to whisker burns?' the doctor asked with a wry grin.

'Yeah, something like that.'

'Sure, I have one you can use. It's in the washroom at the end of the hall and there should be hot water on the stove.'

'Seems like I'm getting farther and farther in debt to you,' he said quietly.

'Like I said, buy me a drink sometime.'

Auggie paced away to the kitchen, picked the whistling kettle up off the stove where the three women were busy with breakfast, walked to the doctor's small washroom, and began lathering up.

He took his time shaving, scraping a full week's worth of whiskers off his

198

face and peering at the not-quite-so-tanned crinkles starting to show at the corners of his eyes in the small mirror.

They used to be laugh lines, he mused, but there'd been precious damned little to laugh about lately.

He wasn't getting any younger, that was for sure, and he wondered if he'd ever have an honest-to-God relationship with a woman like Becky. One he was comfortable with, where he wasn't expecting it to blow up in his face at any minute. One in which it was all right for a couple to show they cared about each other. A wink in a crowded room. A kiss in public. Sharing a laugh, a story, a bed.

He shook his head at the hopelessness of it all.

Becky was right and he knew it. Chances were strong that, if he walked into this gunfight with Keogh's men today, it was never going to happen.

Not to him.

He knew well the emptiness that came from staring into a hundred tiny campfires with no one around to care if he lived or died, no one to call his own, and that was the part of him that no one understood.

He heaved a muffled sigh of frustration and forced himself back to the reality of the moment, drying his face on a rough towel and gazing through the window at the desert behind Sam Curran's place.

There was nothing much out there except rocks and thorns. And the heat, of course.

Always the heat.

Still, it was home.

He'd learned a great deal from the vaqueros he rode with and the few hard-rock miners he'd met while chasing the horse herds, and, in the short time he'd been out here, he'd learned to love the kind of country most people found unlovable.

They called the desert barren and bitter, ugly and arid, ghastly as the gates of hell, and he agreed with them for the most part. Yet, in his heart, he held a secret belief that the terrible desert was rich and full of life, that the ugly was really beautiful, that other people's hell was the one place he belonged.

And it made no sense at all.

★   ★   ★

The saloon was abnormally quiet when Keogh ambled in; a teamster was nursing a shot of whiskey alone at the long bar and a dusty miner slept face down on a table near the door. Shadows hung heavily in every corner and the entire place reeked of pipe smoke.

George Macomber glanced up from behind the bar, stacked a shot glass on a shelf full of dusty brown bottles, and bobbed his head in greeting.

'A little early for you, isn't it, Mister Keogh?'

'Probably so,' Keogh muttered, 'probably so. Is your cook up and at it this early?'

'I can wake her. What'll you have?'

Pushing his bowler hat back on his head, Keogh dropped down to a chair at his usual table and studied the slope-shouldered barman.

'Steak and eggs,' he said, 'whenever she can get around to it. No hurry. I'm going to need a dozen or so men with guns, too, George. Men who are willing to stand guard all afternoon.'

The bartender cocked his head and squinted at him. 'Where's Briscoe and Santee?'

'Kellerman took them down out in the desert. He's on his way here to kill me right now.'

'Kellerman? Isn't he the one who gunned that guy down at your mine?' the barman asked quietly.

'The very one,' Keogh lied.

'Damn! He must be one fast *hombre* with a gun.'

The Copper King wagged his head. 'It wasn't like a regular showdown, you know? More like Injun fighting. Sneaking around the brush and taking pot shots.'

'I was going to say! That Harry Briscoe had taken down some of the fastest gunmen in the West.'

'Can you get me the men or not? The pay will be good and food and drinks are free for anyone who hires on.'

Macomber nodded, glancing up toward the open door. 'I can get them. There are always a few men around who want to turn a few extra bucks.'

'Do you think you can manage to set it up for me, George? I don't know who else I can trust in this burg and you did say you weren't always a bartender. Of course, you'll be well paid, just like the others.'

'Sure, I can set it up,' the barman said quietly. 'Don't worry about that part of it. I've seen my share of trouble, too.'

'I'll want four or five men with rifles covering the front,' Keogh droned, 'four or five covering the back door, and about that many more inside here covering me. And, no matter what else happens, this Kellerman character has got to die.'

Macomber nodded that he understood, started away, then stopped and
turned back. 'You want that steak and
eggs now, Mister Keogh?'

The Copper King leaned back in the
chair, laced his fingers across his belly,
and smiled.

'No hurry, George. I've got all day.'

All day, indeed.

Papago Wells was roughly forty miles
away and it wasn't possible even for
Kellerman to ride in before about
noon.

When he did it would be into a hail
of gunfire such as he'd never even
heard of before.

With a price on his head, he was fair
game for anyone with a gun and he was
going to walk into it as dumb as an owl
at noon.

Only a few more hours and the
Copper King of Arizona could get on
with his life.

He smiled at the thought.

San Francisco in the fall, by God!

Russian Hill, the Embarcadero, the

high-pitched screams of riverboat whistles coming to him through the fog, the subdued chunking of paddle wheels, and the heady aroma of crab cioppino boiling in the big pots that dotted Fisherman's Wharf.

Only a few more hours.

The style of life he wanted, the comfort he longed for, all required money — lots of money — and the only way he could keep it coming in was through the copper on Kellerman's spread.

With Kellerman out of the way there'd be no one to object when he sent his men in there to start mining, no one to raise a fuss over the huge tailing piles that would be left behind, and no one to care about the wildlife he destroyed.

It was, after all, a barren, desolate country.

From what he'd seen, there was enough ore on that little patch of land south of town to keep him in business for several years.

That was exactly what he wanted.

15

The air was crisp and clean, heavy with the orange-blossom and tar fragrance of creosote bushes, the spiny ocotillo plants quickly covering themselves with a fuzz of soft, round leaves and the flames of tiny scarlet flowers blooming at their tips.

It was always so after a rain.

The ominous line of thunderstorms had scudded away to the northwest, billowing whiteness against the brilliant blue of the summer sky, dark cloud shadows drifting across the desert floor, and Auggie stood there for a long moment, just taking it all in.

Times like this were special, and he knew it. Mostly the desert was hazy with dust, everything the color of adobe and dried blood.

A single glance down the street showed him the belted men trickling in through the front door of the saloon and he knew his plan had worked.

He'd caught the Copper King before he could get his defensive barrier set up, before he could select the killing field and get his hired guns in place.

And, even at that, the odds were stacked heavily against him.

There were at least a dozen men in there, every one of them armed to the eye teeth, and every one of them there with only one thought in mind . . .

Kill Auggie Kellerman.

He turned at the soft shuffling of footsteps behind him and stared evenly into the flashing black eyes of Becky Camacho.

Without a word she lay her hand on the corded muscles of his forearm, studying him with obvious questions in her eyes.

'If I make it back,' he said in a hoarse whisper, 'we'll be married this afternoon and head for California. There's nothing left for me here except a bunch of bitter memories.'

'Are you serious?' she asked, tilting her head.

'Yes, I think we've waited long enough.'

She stood on her tiptoes and kissed him fully on the lips. There had been a few other times she'd kissed him, but, somehow, this one was special.

'*Vaya con Dios*, Auggie,' she purred. 'Go with God.'

He locked his fingers in her hair for a moment, lifted her chin for one last kiss, and turned away.

Without another word, he checked the load in the heavy Colt Peacemaker, and stepped down into the narrow street.

It was time.

He walked slowly, deliberately, staying in the shade of the board walkway until he was directly across the street from the saloon, fully aware that with every step he took he was laying his life on the line.

Few people were on the street at this hour; a grizzled shopkeeper was sweeping the porch in front of his store, a miner's wife was sauntering toward home with a sack of groceries for her husband's breakfast, and a slim Mexican boy was loading supplies on to a farm wagon.

None of them seemed aware of the trouble about to erupt in the shaded saloon and Auggie made no move to warn them.

Instead, he angled across the street, tugged the brim of his hat slightly lower, and pushed through the batwing doors as if he were just one more gunhand looking to make a few quick bucks.

The belted men he'd seen entering a few minutes earlier were lined shoulder to shoulder along the bar, splashing quick shots of frontier whiskey into spotty glasses, joking and elbowing each other at the prospect of earning some of Charlie Keogh's money.

He spotted Keogh, smug and confident at a table in the corner; George Macomber, the gregarious barman whom everyone knew, behind the counter and, at the far end of the bar, an old acquaintance of his . . . Deputy US Marshal Jack Raley.

Their eyes locked for an instant across the crowded room but Raley made no move in his direction and Auggie discounted him for the moment, leveling his gaze instead at the self-proclaimed Copper King.

The man he'd come to kill.

'Well, I'll be damned,' Keogh called in a voice loud enough for everyone in the establishment to hear. 'August Kellerman! I didn't expect to see you again this side of the grave.'

His words were meant to alert this bunch of quickly hired gunhands that the man they'd been hired to protect him from had just walked in, but Auggie was way ahead of him.

'And you almost made it,' he said grimly.

A thinly disguised smirk spread across Keogh's lips, his hand conveniently out of sight below the table. Auggie would have bet a month's pay he had an unshucked gun in it.

Keogh wasted no time on the niceties.

The roar of the shot ripped through the stillness that hung over the saloon and splinters of wood exploded into Auggie's face as the bullet tore through the scarred tabletop.

He felt the dry gush of air against his cheek as the shot whined past his head, and he dragged the heavy Peacemaker from its holster in a move so smooth, so fast, it would have made a diamond-back rattler jealous.

The slug took Charlie Keogh squarely in the chest, jerked him violently backwards against the board-and-bat wall of the dimly lit saloon, and he slid to a crumpled heap on the floor, dead before he even came to a stop.

Two more shots thundered out behind him, and Auggie dove to the side, behind a table that had seen better days, twisting quickly to see who was firing.

George Macomber was behind the

bar, and in front of it a dusty teamster was still holding a whiskey glass in his free hand.

Auggie swung the long-barreled Peacemaker up and fired point blank into the teamster's face, saw him reel absurdly back on his heels, and watched the man's pistol flip end over end through the air before it clattered to the floor.

At the far end of the bar Deputy Marshal Raley stepped out of the shadows, brought a sawed-off LeFever shotgun up to bear, squeezed the trigger once, and cut George Macomber down where he stood.

Auggie let go at another teamster who was leveling his gun, drilling him in the chest also, and the gunfight was over almost as quickly as it had started.

Jack Raley took a step away from the bar, pushed his frock coat open, making the six-pointed marshal's star plainly visible to everyone in the place, and let the scattergun in his hard hands sweep the room.

'That's the end of it, boys,' he announced.

'There's no one left to pay you now.'

'There's still a reward out for him,' another teamster replied, nodding toward Auggie.

'No, the man who's guilty of murder here is lying dead over there in the corner.'

'Charlie Keogh?' the teamster asked incredulously.

'He's the one. I've got an eyewitness to the shooting of Ram Garza, who swore an affidavit to it this morning.

'Kellerman was wrongly accused and wrongly convicted. He's not guilty of a damned thing except running a crew of hard-working mustang men.'

The deputy set the scattergun carefully down on the bar and surveyed the crowd of would-be gun-hands yet again.

'If you really want to collect some reward money,' he ventured, 'this guy calling himself George Macomber, behind the bar there, is really George Butler Bryan — I recognize him from the wanted posters on him back in

Texas — and there's a sizable piece of change being offered on his head. And, from what George told me before he met his maker, you'll find the bodies of Harry Briscoe and a hardcase named Santee down at Papago Wells. They were both wanted in Texas and I'm pretty sure there's some money out on them, too.'

'Yeah?' the teamster ventured. 'Well, that ends it for me. There's no way in hell I'm riding all the way back to Texas to collect on a couple of measly damned rewards. I ain't quite that desperate. You fellers want it, it's all yours.'

He threw down the rest of his whiskey, wiped a dusty sleeve across his mouth, and walked out. Fully half the men who'd crowded into the shadowed Ajo saloon followed his lead.

Just as the line of hard-faced men were trooping out, he saw his bride-to-be, little Becky Camacho, push her way through the batwing doors and step inside.

Out of pure respect, the men stood aside and let her pass.

He noted the appraising looks they lavished on her as she marched past and couldn't blame them for a minute. She had somehow found time to change into a burgundy skirt, a spotless white blouse, and had tied her hair up in an enticing ponytail.

She was beautiful.

Her eyes darted around the dark interior of the room, finally settling on him just as he was picking himself up from behind the splintered table, holstering the big Peacemaker. She hurried into his arms.

'Are you all right?' she asked quickly.

'I think so,' he murmured, 'but it was a close thing.'

'You're not hit?'

'No. I got a face full of slivers but no bullet holes.'

A tired sigh escaped her lips and she pressed herself close against him. 'Thank God. I was so worried.'

Auggie lifted his gaze to Deputy Raley with a respect he hadn't felt before.

'How'd you know where I'd be?' he asked quietly.

'It wasn't hard to figure. You wouldn't have come back if you didn't have something to prove.'

Auggie nodded his understanding at the deputy's reasoning and asked the question that had plagued him since seeing him in here.

'So what now?'

Raley shook his head uncertainly and lifted his hands. 'I don't know, Auggie. You've got me between a rock and a hard place. By law I've got to take you in, but I heard enough from a guy named Gil Torres this morning to know you got railroaded by a crooked judge and I just don't want to play anymore.'

He exhaled heavily, tipped another shot of whiskey into his glass, and continued.

'Do me a favor and head for California . . . Nevada, maybe . . . but get the hell out of the Territory so I don't have to earn my pay. I don't know why I should, but I'm going to Tucson when I leave here to get this murder conviction against you dropped once and for all.'

'You'd do that for me?'

'I'll try,' Raley mumbled. 'I may lose my job over it, but I'll try. I think if I'd been in your shoes back there, knowing full well I was innocent, I'd probably have done the same thing.'

'And there'll be no more reward out on my head? I can get on with my life?'

'No reason not to. It looks to me like you and this little beauty here already have a few plans along that line.'

'A few,' Auggie agreed, cutting his eyes over to Becky.

'One question before I head out,' the deputy said, throwing down the rest of his whiskey.

'What's that?'

'Those other two prisoners, Melnick and Davis, any idea where they headed?'

'They're dead. Jumped us on the trail west of Papago Wells and weren't quite as slick as they thought they were. My foreman cut the half-breed down with a shotgun and the last I saw of Melnick, he had a nasty .45 caliber hole in his chest and was being dragged toward the Mohawk Mountains by a spooked horse.'

'If you'll swear to that,' the deputy droned, 'I won't have to go looking for them.'

'Of course I'll swear to it. Didn't like those two from the giddyup. And, Jack? If you do lose your job over this, I can always use an honest ranch hand out in Monterey.'

'California?'

'That's our plan right now. Ask around up by the Mission San Juan Bautista. That's where we'll be for a while.'

Raley nodded soberly, set his shot glass down, and stepped away from the bar. 'I guess that winds it up for me, then.'

'What about the horse?'

'You keep her,' the deputy rumbled. 'I never liked that hammerhead much anyway.'

'I don't know, she saved my bacon a couple of times out there.'

The deputy chuckled half under his breath. 'She must like you, Auggie. For sure and for certain she never did a damned thing for me.'

'And the gun?' he asked.

'Call it a gift. I've already got another one.'

'What about the lump I put on the back of your head?'

Raley grunted deep in his throat at the question, jerked a big fist up suddenly from somewhere down around the knees, and knocked Auggie flat on his ass on the saloon's rough-sawn floor.

'We'll call it even on that score,' he said evenly.

He turned on his heel, paced across to the open door, and stepped out into the dry Arizona morning.

Without a word Auggie propped himself up on his elbow as Becky knelt close by his side, wiped the blood off his lip with the back of his hand, and grinned at Jack Raley's broad back.

He really wasn't a bad guy, as far as US marshals went.

And, yeah, Auggie Kellerman figured he'd had that one coming.

THE END

We do hope that you have enjoyed reading this large print book.

Did you know that all of our titles are available for purchase?

We publish a wide range of high quality large print books including:
**Romances, Mysteries, Classics
General Fiction
Non Fiction and Westerns**

Special interest titles available in large print are:
**The Little Oxford Dictionary
Music Book, Song Book
Hymn Book, Service Book**

Also available from us courtesy of Oxford University Press:
**Young Readers' Dictionary
(large print edition)
Young Readers' Thesaurus
(large print edition)**

For further information or a free brochure, please contact us at:
**Ulverscroft Large Print Books Ltd.,
The Green, Bradgate Road, Anstey,
Leicester, LE7 7FU, England.
Tel:** (00 44) **0116 236 4325**
Fax: (00 44) **0116 234 0205**

Other titles in the
Linford Western Library:

SHERIFF WITHOUT A STAR

I. J Parnham

Cassidy Yates had been stripped of his Sheriff's star by the townsfolk of Monotony. Leland Matlock's son had died, due to his error of judgement. Then Leland, ready to reveal information that could have shed new light on the sheriff's downfall, was shot. Cassidy believed that Leland's shooting was connected to the death of his son. So, rising to the challenge to uncover the link, Cassidy endeavoured to get that star pinned back on his chest where it belonged.

THE DEVIL'S PAYROLL

Paul Green

When bounty hunter John Harrison captures fugitive outlaw Clay Barton, he's persuaded by Maggie Sloane to allow the captive to lead them to the loot robbed from an army payroll. But Barton double-crosses them and the mysterious Leo Gabriel kidnaps Maggie. With a veteran Buffalo Soldier, Sergeant Eli Johnson, at his side, Harrison battles ruthless vaqueros and a Comanche war party to recover the money, re-capture Barton and rescue Maggie . . . but a surprise awaits him when he finally catches up with his enemies . . .

HELL ON HOOFS

Lance Howard

Arriving in Lancerville, John Laramie hoped to escape his old life as a man-hunter and settle down. But there he finds he's torn between the demons of his past and hope for a brighter future when a young woman seeks his help in getting rid of a vicious outlaw. Then the Cross Gang attacks him and the young woman's life is put in danger. But will it cost Laramie more to win than to lose in a deadly showdown?

TROUBLE AT MESQUITE FLATS

Will Keen

Arriving in Mesquite Flats, ex-New York businessman Bodene Rich is committed to Yuma Penitentiary for a vicious assault. He's released, in light of new evidence, and pardoned by Warden Bradley Shaw. On the day of Rich's release, Shaw resigns, but an unknown gunman then shoots him dead on the trail. Rich once again is in trouble. And, in a showdown, he's embroiled in a bloody gun battle, where the outcome hangs in the balance until the final shot . . .

HELL STAGE TO LONE PINE

Jack Dakota

At Lone Pine Ranch, young Ben Brewer wants to prove himself to the owner, Morgan Hethridge and his beautiful daughter Josie. But Hethridge's rival is scheming to take over Lone Pine ranch. To protect the land, Brewer faces the feared gunhawk Calvin Choate. A desperate situation, until old timer Whipcrack Riley steps in. Will his wily ways and his skills driving a stagecoach be enough to help Brewer once the situation gets really rough and the bullets are flying?